CONTENT WARNING

This book includes the following triggers. Skip to avoid possible spoilers.

Dubious consent scenarios, implied domestic abuse & violence, Amnesia & memory disorders, Childbirth, Medical experimentation, Scars, Grief & loss depiction, Murder & attempted murder, Fire & arson.

I have tried to handle these dark themes with compassion and grace. Your mental health matters more than any book.

Love and light,

Jennifer L. Hart

MY MIDLIFE MAGIC DAZE

JENNIFER L. HART

ELEMENTS UNLEASHED MEDIA

PAGES AND POTIONS
BOOK 1

My Midlife Magic Daze

Hart/ Jennifer L.

1.Women's—Fiction 2. North Carolina—Fiction 3. Paranormal—Fiction 4. Witch Romance—Fiction 5. Demons Romance—Fiction 6. Amnesia—Fiction 7. Small Towns—Fiction 8. Mystery—Fiction 9. American Humorous—Fiction 10.Mountain Living — Fiction 11. Secret Baby— Fiction 12. Magic—Fiction I. Title

ISBN: 978-1-965136-15-7

MY MIDLIFE MAGIC DAZE

PROLOGUE

The light drew me forward. Not an ordinary light. A sign. I read the flickering hot pink letters behind the glass even as the icy rain pummeled my uncovered head and plastered wet strands of dark hair against my face. The words blurred with the pain in my midsection, but I clung to the scripted scrawl like a lifeline.

Pages & Potions.

The sign flickered on and off, then on again as though it was winking at me, trying to grab my attention. The inconsistent illumination cast eerie shadows against the wet sidewalk. I stumbled towards it like a moth drawn to a flame. Like the moth, I didn't care if the light burned me, if it guided me out of the darkness.

A small bell jingled above the door as I pushed it inward. The wet weather blew at my back, almost like it didn't want to admit defeat. Even though the sign was on, and the door unlocked, the overhead lights powered down. Large rectangular shelves lined the far walls. Lumps of assorted sizes were scattered haphazardly throughout the low-ceilinged space. Furniture perhaps.

The place smelled of herbs and spices, as well as that indescribable allure of hundreds upon hundreds of books.

No signs of life.

"Hello?" My voice, unfamiliar, came out as a warbling croak.

"We're closed!" A woman hollered from somewhere to my left.

I shuffled forward, conscious that I was trailing water across the hardwood floor. "Please. I need...help."

"Thought I locked that damn door. Does this look like a police station to you?" The cantankerous voice called out. "I ain't no fricking doctor and I don't much appreciate—"

The overhead light flared to life at the same time the light in the window died. I threw a hand up to shield my eyes from the sudden brightness.

"Oh, my word." The woman's tone had changed from cranky to shocked. "Rue, get down here!"

"Please," I begged again, unsure what I asked her for. Keeping my eyes shielded, I drank in her features. Skin thin as parchment, wrinkled from sun and time. Her eyes were a vivid blue though and were lit with sharp intelligence.

Footsteps sounded on the curved stairs to my right. Another woman, smaller and rounder than the first, with fewer wrinkles, paused on the landing. She had the same wide blue eyes, though hers were hidden behind thick glasses. She wore a ratty pink bathrobe and slippers. "What's all the fuss about—?"

She too cut off when her gaze landed on me. She swayed in place until I thought she'd tumble down the stairs. Only a white-knuckled grip on the banister kept her in place. "I'll call 911."

"No." I reached out a hand as though I could stop her from moving. "Please. I don't want anyone else to know that I'm here."

"Honey," the woman on the stairs began. "You're soaked in blood."

I stared at her, unable to deny the truth. "Please."

The women exchanged a speaking glance. Then the first one drew in a deep

breath. "Come on into the kitchen and let us get a better look at you."

My shoulders slumped in relief. I followed obediently as the woman headed down a narrow hall to a small kitchen. Shuffling footsteps told me the one on the stairs—Rue—trailed behind.

The overhead light in the kitchen was even more glaring than the one in the front room. It bounced off dingy linoleum and battle-scarred wood cabinets with almost blinding intensity.

"I'm Hatty Bramblewick," the taller of the two said

3

as she dragged out a heavy metal chair and gestured for me to sit. "This is my sister, Rue Bramblewick."

"Pleased to meet you both," I murmured.

"What's your name, honey?" Rue pushed her glasses farther up her nose as she looked me over for other signs of injury.

My lips parted, but no sound came out. My brows drew together. "I don't...that is...I'm not sure...?"

Another speaking glance was exchanged between them. They were wondering if they could believe me. It sounded nuts. What sort of person just appeared out of the ether, bleeding, and with no identity?

"Please," I swallowed.

"We've got towels in the dryer," Hatty grumbled after a pause. "Let's get you out of those wet things."

My hands shook so hard I had trouble undoing the buttons on my shirt. Rue stepped forward and brushed my hands aside. She peeled the stained linen from me and held it away from herself with two fingers as Hatty returned with a warm, white towel.

I flinched when my sticky red hands reached for the pristine terrycloth. "I'll ruin it."

"Pish," Hatty waved it away. "I'd rather replace a few towels than watch you shiver to death in front of me."

I took the towel and began to dry my hair. The fabric was warm and soothing, much like the light in the window. The ache in my midsection was growing worse, though. My skin felt too tight, as though it was shrinking. Shivering, I slumped against the side of the kitchen table.

Rue fussed with a kettle full of hot water. "What happened to you, dear?"

Another question I didn't have the answer to, so I whispered, "I'm not sure."

Hatty crouched on the floor and pulled sneakers off my sockless feet. "This is no way to go about in such nasty weather. You don't even have a coat."

My teeth were chattering too hard to reply. I buried my face in the towel, trying to soak up its warmth. *So cold.*

"Stand up," Hatty ordered. "We need to get those pants off before you catch your death."

It took all my strength to brace against the table. I pushed myself to stand and wavered.

"Come help me hold her up," Hatty barked. Rue scurried to obey. The meeker sister only came up to my chin, while Hatty could look me in the eye.

How tall am I? The thought flitted through my mind and then vanished into the foggy depths.

With businesslike fingers, Hatty unfastened my jeans and then pushed the zipper down. She sucked in a breath when the skin beneath came into view.

"Hatty..." Rue's voice quavered.

"I see it. Mother Moon, I see it."

"What?" I glanced down to see what had caught their attention.

Jagged black threads held together what remained of my abdomen, the pale

5

flesh oozing pinkish fluid. My hand drifted down but didn't make contact. Most of the blood was coming from between my legs.

"We really should get you to the hospital," Hatty breathed.

"No, please." I gripped her arm as instinct cautioned me to tread carefully. "They'll call the police."

Blue eyes met mine. "Someone butchered you, child. This isn't something that should be hidden away."

My entire body trembled from fear, and cold, but I shook my head. I'd brought trouble to these strangers. "I'll go."

"Stubborn," Hatty muttered and then bent low, dragging the wet denim down my long legs. "You might be hemorrhaging."

"What about Grayson?" Rue wrung her hands. "He could look. Let us know if she'll be all right?"

Hatty sniffed but then nodded. "Call him. You, girl, sit down before you fall down." The last part was directed at me.

I was pushed back into the chair but couldn't hold my seat. Gravity sank her claws in and dragged me to the floor. My lids felt too heavy. I gave up the fight to remain conscious.

I awoke to the sound of rain pelting against the glass. An elderly man with a puff of white hair and hands gnarled from arthritis sat in the chair beside my bed. He smiled when he noticed me looking. "Good morning. You gave us quite a scare."

"I'm sorry."

"Oh, quit apologizing already," a familiar voice snapped from behind me. "It's not like you asked someone to carve you up like the Christmas Goose."

I shifted, wincing as the motion pulled at my wrecked stomach muscles. Hatty stood there, glaring not at me but at the man with the cotton-white hair.

He didn't wilt under her scrutiny, though. Instead, he reached out and took my wrist with one hand. "Her pulse is strong and steady. I'm going to write you a prescription for iron supplements as well as the antibiotics." His drawl was distinctly southern, rounding out the vowels as he spoke.

"Write them in my name," Hatty ordered. "We don't know if she has insurance."

He nodded and then reached for his bag. "Walk me out, will you?"

"Hmph," Hatty grunted but then reached out and squeezed my shoulder. Her tone softened as she murmured, "I'll be right back."

I listened to their low conversation in the hall. They tried to keep their voices down, but every word carried through the thin walls.

"Will she be all right?" That was Hatty's voice. I recognized the crisp way she spoke, as though words were her weapon of choice.

A pause and then the man drawled, "She's healthy, other than the botched C-section. The bastards that operated didn't remove all the placenta. I got it out and sutured her properly. I'm amazed whoever did that to her bothered to stitch her up at all."

Grayson cleared his throat before he continued. "Hatty, you don't know anything about this woman. You and Rue have no clue what you're getting yourselves into by taking her in."

"I know she came to us for help." Hatty's tone was unyielding. "If the universe saw fit to deliver her to our doorstep, then we have a responsibility to help her."

There was a pause. "You know I ought to report this."

"You had your chance to do that last night," Hatty growled. "What will you tell them now? That you performed an illegal operation on a strange woman in my kitchen?"

"In for a penny, in for a pound. That's how it always is with you." There was a smile in the man's voice. "Okay, let me call Ronald and get you those prescriptions."

Their footsteps receded down the stairs.

Again, my hand drifted down to my sore midsection. A C-section? Had I given birth? Was there a baby somewhere out there with half my DNA? Why couldn't I remember anything?

Panic clawed at me and my hand shot out, connecting with the wall behind the wrought iron bed. Instead of being smooth, it was constructed of bark shingles. The rough texture scraped my palm as I made contact.

Be at ease. You're safe.

That voice. Deep, rich, masculine. It seeped through my pores and slid along my bones. My eyes slid shut, and I took a shuddering breath. I must be hallucinating. No one else was in the room.

Still, I kept my hand on the wall, unwilling to break the contact until the door to my room opened. Rue appeared, holding a tea tray. "Good morning, Sunshine."

Though my head felt stuffed full of cotton wool, I greeted the small, round woman who had a much softer voice than her no-nonsense sister. "Thank you so much for everything."

"You're very welcome." She shuffled in and put the tray down on the dresser. "I have a rosehip, lemon balm, and hibiscus herbal blend for you to try. It helps with women's problems."

She helped me struggle upright and propped pillows behind me before pouring me a steaming mug full of the fragrant brew. It had a light floral flavor. I drank it down greedily. "It's delicious."

Rue beamed. "I'm glad you like it. I'm thinking

about putting it on the menu downstairs. Hatty hates it, but she's a coffee drinker, so her palate can't be trusted."

The image of the sign stuck out in my mind. *Pages & Potions.* "What exactly do you do downstairs?"

Rue blinked owlishly. "Oh, why we're a bookshop and a café. When we inherited the house from our grandmother, we needed a way to pay for the upkeep. Hatty wanted a bookstore, and I wanted a café. So we compromised."

I looked around the room where I'd been deposited. "And is this your room?"

She shook her head. "No, dear. I'm across the hall. Hatty is downstairs in Grammy's old room. This is a guest space. You're welcome to stay for as long as you like."

My lips trembled. I hadn't given any thought to what came next. I'd been surviving from moment to moment with no plan. Her offer touched me beyond words.

The heavy thump of footsteps on the stairs made me glance toward the door. A moment later, Hatty reappeared. "What foul brew did she give you?"

"*She* likes my tea," Rue said acidly. "Because unlike you, *she* has good taste."

Hatty rolled her eyes. "She needs a name other than she. A name and a story that people will be able to get their heads around."

"What do you mean?" I whispered.

Rue took my hand and squeezed while Hatty

explained, "Mist Glen is a tiny village. Everybody here knows everybody else. And for sport, they tend to get up in each other's business. I'm not sure if the monsters that hurt you are looking for you, but if you want to stay hidden, you need a cover story."

"A believable cover story," Rue added. "Just until your memories come back."

"Will they?" I whispered.

Hatty's direct gaze put me at ease. "Grayson couldn't say. Only that it doesn't look like you hit your head. He doesn't know why you can't remember anything, never mind if your memories will return."

I nodded slowly.

"So, a name," Hatty continued. "What about Rose? Or Elaine? Cheryl?"

My hand once again covered my battered midsection.

"Emma," Rue murmured.

I met her soft blue gaze.

Her smile wobbled as she added, "It means whole."

"Emma," I repeated and then drew in a deep breath. "Okay."

"Emma Bishop," Hatty said. "Our cousin from Memphis."

"Emma Bishop from Memphis." I nodded. "Where are we now?"

"Mist Glen." Hatty said and at my blank look added, "We're in the northwesternmost county of North Carolina, about 3,000 feet above sea level."

I shut my eyes and digested the news. Tried to picture anything about the area. Nothing before the sign for the bookstore registered. My memory banks sat empty.

"We better go and let you get some rest, Cousin Emma." Hatty shuffled toward the door and Rue followed suit, collecting the tea tray.

After settling back down between the covers, one hand pressed against the wall, I watched the rain fall. This house was a safe place to rest for the time being. All I could do was hope my memory returned in time.

And that I found my missing child.

Death doesn't stop people from being assholes.

Out of the corner of my eye, I kept track of the woman browsing the children's section while the ghost of her late husband shouted at her.

"How dare you sell my car! Do you know how much I paid for the vintage seat covers?" His meaty hands clenched into fists and though his face was the same sallow mist color as the rest of his insubstantial form, I thought if he'd been alive instead of a spirit, he would have been red in the face.

The woman's wardrobe consisted of a nappy polar fleece hoodie over a long-sleeved V-neck and well-worn jeans that sported holes from long-term wear instead of a designer's whim. Her once-white sneakers were stained, the laces mismatched as though one had broken. Going by her clothing and the fact that she was pawing through the used bin, she had bigger problems than a deceased mantrum.

Ghosts often didn't know they had crossed the veil that separated life from the afterlife or that they were no longer ensconced in the land of the living. If I hadn't been working on frothing a latte, I might have pulled the bastard aside and explained a few things to him. Like that, he was a spirit and had no use for an expensive car. Status symbols didn't mean anything to the deceased. His wife was doing the best she could without him. I wished he would cross over and quit damaging the calm in *Pages & Potions*.

Even if I was the only one aware of him.

"Almost done, Emma?" Hatty perched on the middle stool in front of the counter. A laptop sat open in front of her. Her cat-eye readers perched on the end of her sharp blade of a nose. She peered at me over the top of them. Hatty knew I could see ghosts. She was the one who'd warned me not to reveal my gift in front of anyone else. It was all part of my hiding-in-plain-sight act.

"Mmm hmmm." I turned my back on the pissed-off apparition and presented the foam-topped beverage to Milly Banks. Milly was a regular who came in every week to trundle through the new release section and treat herself to a latte and whatever baked good had come out of Rue's kitchen that morning. Today's special was banana walnut bread. The second I smelled it baking, I'd written it on the chalkboard in the window next to the defunct sign. Hatty had a habit of buying bananas that she never ate, so the bread was Rue's way of utilizing the past its prime fruit. *Waste not, want not,* was her mantra.

Without asking, I cut two slices from the loaf and put them on a white dessert plate. Snack in hand, I headed to the register while the ghost kept up his tirade.

"Oh, I shouldn't." Milly eyed the bread like a starving woman. "Doc Trammel has me on a low-carb diet."

"That is low carb," Hatty lied without batting an eyelash.

"Really?" Milly's Southern drawl stretched the two syllables out into infinity.

"It's as healthy as banana nut bread gets," I supplied. Rue was experimenting with her baking by removing trans fats and sugar wherever she could without sacrificing flavor. Whether the doctor would agree was a different matter.

"Oh, I guess this once won't hurt anything." Milly caved the way she always did. She fished in her wallet for a five-dollar bill and paid for her snack.

After ringing up the purchase, I thanked her. Once she was seated in a wingback chair in the new release section, I hissed at Hatty, "Banana nut bread isn't low carb."

"Did you *want* to stand here all day listening to her bemoan her diet?" Hatty arched one thin brow.

"No." Mother Moon preserve us. Nothing was

more grueling than listening to people ramble on about food they couldn't or shouldn't eat.

Hatty nodded crisply. "Well, there you go. I expedited the process. No thanks required. Now quit staring at that woman before you give her a complex."

"She's got a tagalong." I used our codeword for a ghost who followed the living into Glimmer Ridge.

Hatty grunted. "There's nothing you can do, Emma. Best leave them be."

She was right. As I took the milk cup over to the sink to wash, I acknowledged the reality. There wasn't a single thing I could do about the ghosts. Every time I'd tried, the situation went from bad to worse. The departed's loved ones thought I was nuts. Or some sort of con artist hunting for a payday. More than one door had been slammed in my face. Plus, the ghosts pestered me for days after they realized I could see them. They hung around night and day because another fun fact about the dead, they never needed to sleep.

Having a demanding ghost standing by my bed and yammering at me all night wasn't an experience I wanted to repeat.

Plus, I was supposed to be keeping a low profile. Alerting people that I could see their tagalongs was the opposite of going unnoticed.

Hatty removed her glasses, letting them dangle on the gold chain around her neck. She stood to stretch out her back. "I've got the register. Why don't you go sweep the front porch and the walkway?"

Nodding, I shucked my apron, balled it up beneath the counter, and then headed to the closet by the front door to retrieve the outdoor broom.

Hatty and Rue were very serious about brooms. It went along with their witchy beliefs. According to the Bramblewick sisters, one should never use an outdoor broom in an indoor space and vice versa. It didn't make a lick of sense to me. However, they'd given me so much over the last five years that I did what they asked, no matter how silly it sounded.

Stepping onto the large porch, I looked out at the mist-enshrouded village. Mist Glen—population 1,243 —had been built in the lowest part of the valley, surrounded by craggy peaks. The fog had a habit of spilling down over the rough terrain and settling in the bowl-like valley the way frothed milk poured into a mug. The mist often lasted until midmorning, snaking between buildings like a cat weaving between its owner's legs until the sun crested the peaks and chased it away. The village was the only home I could remember, just like the house—Glimmer Ridge.

Technically speaking, Glimmer Ridge predated the village. Classic Linville architecture that combined one-part Swiss chalet with one-part Appalachian mountain. Built from the extinct Chestnut tree in 1922, Glimmer Ridge sported bark shingles inside and out. Over the years, it had been passed from owner to owner in a game of hot potato, each person taking on an aging structure that grew tougher to care for as the years passed.

Until Rue and Hatty Bramblewick inherited Glimmer Ridge.

I'd seen pictures from the early days—missing shingles, a sagging porch, and a crumbling foundation. Twenty years ago, the house had been on the verge of being condemned. The Bramblewicks had managed to turn the place around. The repairs were made using Poplar bark since the Chestnut Blight had taken out the original tree. The sisters worked tirelessly to restore the place to its original glory. A labor of love and foolishness, Hatty claimed.

The front door, situated steps off Main Street, welcomed patrons with classic Southern hospitality. The house boasted a large porch lined with rocking chairs that invited shoppers to stay for a spell. A vaulted ceiling with exposed log beams trapped the sultry summer heat while lazy fans circled overhead. Large windows with failed seals meant we shivered in the winter, but at least the view across the square toward the slow-moving New River was pretty.

Hatty was a fan of home renovation shows. When we watched, the sisters often commented on how nice it would be to update the house to more modern standards. The dicey wiring, the crappy weather stripping around the doors and windows, the dated kitchen that was barely functional. The stove was original and good enough for Rue to bake. The ancient water heater proved temperamental and hot showers were more a pleasant surprise than a constant. No matter the flaws, though, Glimmer Ridge was the only home I could remember.

My life before the night I'd met Hatty and Rue remained a total blank. It made zero sense. No one in town had ever recognized me. To my knowledge, no one had come looking. The story that I was a young cousin of the Bramblewicks had become my reality. Hatty claimed the Bishops were their family's equivalent of the Sackville-Bagginses—the less imaginative branch of the family tree, often embarrassed by their witchy cousins. In other words, no one would refute my claim.

The mystery of where I'd come from went unsolved. No public transportation stopped in Mist Glen, and no major roads passed through. During the autumn, the village swelled with leaf-peeping tourists who'd stop by *Abe's Diner* for a bite before hopping back onto the Blue Ridge Parkway. But most didn't realize Mist Glen existed. So how had I found it?

Rue claimed it was fate. As part of a local coven of witches, the sisters believed in the occult. They accepted me and didn't mind that I saw ghosts. They kept me safe. While I appreciated the family I'd found with the eccentric Bramblewicks, I still craved answers.

A gust of February wind numbed the hands that clutched the straw broom. After sweeping from east to west—the way Hatty claimed was proper—I leaned the broom against the door. Ignoring the rocking chairs, I lowered myself onto the top step, pressing my back against a vertical log, and wished my curiosity away. It was dangerous to want more. The fear that had coursed through my bloodstream on the night I'd come to Glimmer Ridge remained potent in my mind. Remembered terror made my heart race and the world cave in around me.

Shutting my eyes, I leaned back against the log support that held the roof over the covered porch, pressing my body firmly against the house. Just like that first morning after my fever broke, I felt the calm, protective presence coming from the house. It seeped into me like sunlight, warming all the cold places inside me, caressing and comforting, and staving off a panic attack. As if the rough bark was a conduit, that same dark voice echoed in my mind.

You're safe. Everything will be all right.

Slowly, my breathing evened out. There was no way to describe the reassurance I received whenever I touched the house. It was almost as though Glimmer Ridge wrapped me in invisible arms as that resonant voice filled with smoke and shadows vowed to protect me.

The door behind me jingled and the woman in the holey jeans strode down the steps toward the street. My lips curled up as I spotted a wrapped loaf of banana nut bread in her hand. Hatty was such a softy, but only when she thought no one else was looking. The tagalong drifted through the wall, still bitching at her. When our gazes met, she gave me a weary smile before hurrying down to climb into her battered

Hyundai Santa Fe. Even if she couldn't hear the diatribe from her deceased husband, no one deserved to be talked to that way when all she wanted was to buy a book for her kid.

"Back off, pal," I muttered to the ghost when I felt sure the woman couldn't hear me. "She's doing the best she can. So just cross over already."

The apparition's mouth snapped shut. He pivoted in place on the sidewalk and looked directly at me. Had he heard me? I hadn't spoken loudly.

The echo of his eyes went wide, and his mouth dropped open as he gaped at me. My brows drew down in confusion. What was his problem?

Before I could say anything, though, he wavered a moment, like an old-fashioned television channel blurring out of focus. Then he vanished.

"Weird," I muttered. Shrugging it off, I got to my feet, collected the outdoor broom, and headed back into the store.

When it came to *Pages & Potions*, weird was standard practice.

"Oh no," Rue breathed as she set the newspaper down. "Jody Haversham is missing."

"Who's Jody Haversham?" Hatty didn't bother looking up from her computer screen.

Rue tsked, "Oh honestly, Hatty. You remember Jody. He comes in every now and then and pokes around the occult section. Lives in that apartment above Mrs. Otis's barn. I hope he's all right." Rue pushed her chair out, but I gestured for her to stay where she was and set about collecting our dinner plates.

"He probably took off with some floozy." Hatty's pale eyebrows formed a steep V over her sharp nose, her attention fixed on her spreadsheet.

"I don't think he's the sort, not if you're talking about the man I'm thinking of," I added and turned the hot water tap at the sink, hoping it would cooperate. "Mid-sixties, about five foot eleven, walked with a cane. All white hair and twinkling blue eyes. He was a gentleman, always tipped well when I got him a coffee."

Staring at my reflection in the window above the sink, I wondered how someone would describe me on a missing bulletin. Mid-forties, brunette, with eyes that looked green when I wore green and blue when I wore blue. Average bust, larger than the average backside. Classic pear shape. Easy to overlook. No tattoos or piercings other than a single hole in each ear. Nothing special. No identifying features that would make me stand out in a crowd.

Sometimes I wondered if I blended in *too* well.

You're perfect, Glimmer Ridge whispered in my mind, making me fumble with a sudsy skillet.

There was a unique feature. The house talked to

me. More than that, it made me *feel*. At times, it was a comforting presence. And late at night, that rich, smoky voice sent a shiver through me that had nothing to do with fear.

I'd told the Bramblewick sisters about how Glimmer Ridge spoke to me—leaving out the odd sexual thrill—hoping they knew something about it. They'd exchanged another of those long, loaded looks that meant I'd stumbled into unknown territory.

"There are such things as spirits of the house," Hatty had said at length. "Oftentimes, a house will take on characteristics of its inhabitants. It's why you should always treat your dwelling with respect."

"But if Glimmer Ridge is a spirit, why can't I see him?" I'd asked.

"Who knows, sweets?" Rue had done a one-arm shrug and changed the subject.

Long story short—they thought I was nuts to believe Glimmer Ridge was a person. And that was coming from the coven elders. Peachy.

"How do they know he's missing?" Hatty asked, breaking me from my reverie.

"Mrs. Otis said he didn't pay his rent the first of the month. All his stuff is there, including his car," Rue fretted. "The police are looking into it. Speaking of the police..."

Her gaze slid to me, and I barely bit back a groan. *Not again.*

"Deputy Harding stopped by when you went to the

bank earlier," Rue spoke in a tone that made my spine shoot straight. "He was asking about you."

"Was he?" I whispered faintly.

Art Harding was one of the seven single men under seventy in Mist Glen. Rue loved nothing more than playing matchmaker.

"Yup. He asked if you might want to go to the movies with him sometime." Her tone was just a little too casual to be believed.

"Rue," Hatty began, "She's not interested."

"Well, why not?" Rue huffed. "Emma needs to get out more. And he's such a nice young man."

Hatty made a gagging noise. "Kiss of death right there. You might as well tell her he has a great personality. Besides, since when does Emma need a man?"

"She doesn't need one, but maybe she wants one." Rue sniffed. "And he's been carrying a torch for Emma since she came here."

Hatty shut the laptop with a snick. "And doesn't that strike you as a little odd? Why can't he sniff around a woman who wants him back and leave our girl alone?"

Rue planted her hands on her substantial hips. "Just because you're an old sourpuss when it comes to affairs of the heart doesn't mean Emma's in the same boat."

"Well, why don't you ask Emma?" Hatty snapped in a tone that brooked no nonsense. "Let her decide for herself if she's interested in the man."

Two graying heads swung in my direction. I hated

it when the sisters fought, especially if it had anything to do with me. "I'm not sure I'm ready to date. Can I think about it?"

"Oh, of course, sweets. No pressure." Rue was the soul of understanding as she picked up a tea towel and began to dry.

Hatty just smirked and opened her laptop once more.

Rue chatted about the upcoming full moon revel being held two towns over and who she expected would turn up. I finished washing the dishes and then headed out into the store to go through the closing routine. First, I locked the front door. The sign hadn't worked since the night I'd arrived at *Pages & Potions*, so there was nothing to flick off. Next, I wiped down the counters and set up the coffee and tea service for the following day. I strode through the bookshelves with a microfiber cloth, eliminating dust and hunting for anything out of place. The children's section, the room that once upon a time had been a sitting room over-looking the front yard, typically required the most straightening.

I plugged in the vacuum and pushed the ancient thing over the world map rug and then arranged the bean bag chairs and oversized pillows. We had the kindergarten class coming in for story hour the following day, and I wanted everything to be perfect.

After stowing the vacuum, I paused to admire the mural I'd done of the *Jolly Roger* drifting among the stars on an interior wall, one of the few that wasn't shingled. If I was proud of anything over the last five years, it was that mural. Would the child I'd given birth to like *Peter Pan* as much as I did?

My hand covered my scar, right over the ache that throbbed deep inside whenever I thought of my baby. The not knowing chipped away at me day by day. Had my child survived? Somehow, I didn't think I was supposed to. Who had done that to me? To us?

Frazzled, I turned around to replace a handful of bodice-ripper romances, which definitely didn't belong in that room and almost walked into him.

Or rather, *through* him.

"Mother Moon." A hand flew to my chest as I studied the ghost. Roughly five feet eleven inches tall, with a shock of white hair, he held a cane. His once blue gaze appeared muted, along with his chalky pallor. The intensity that I recalled remained and it fixed on me.

"Emma," the ghost of Jody Haversham murmured. "I need your help."

TWO

T he books fell from my numb fingers. "How did you know...?"

"That you could see the dead?" Jody smiled the same crooked smile he'd had in life. "I've been watching you for a while. But your interaction with the ghost today confirmed my suspicions."

I shook my head. "You saw him too?" It's not like ghosts congregated together to chit-chat. It was rare that I saw them, rarer still to come across two in one day. The only time I had, it had been a set of twin girls who'd followed their younger brother in for story hour. They hadn't said a word to him or each other. I learned later that they'd all been in a car accident together, but only the boy and his dad had survived.

Unlike the entitled asshole from earlier, Mr. Haversham *understood* that he was dead.

"You can see other ghosts?" I asked. "Hear them?"

He nodded. "That one today was a real piece of

work. Makes you wonder if the wife isn't better off without him."

Not knowing what else to do, I crouched down and retrieved the romance novels I'd dropped. "There's nothing I can do for you, Mr. Haversham. No one believed me the few times I tried to deliver a message."

"Call me Jody. And all I need is for you to let people know that I'm gone."

"Emma?" Hatty called from the main room. "Are you all right?"

I stared at the ghost and called out, "Yeah. Be right there."

"Tell them," Mr. Haversham—Jody urged. "They haven't even found my body yet. I think I'm stuck here until they bury me properly."

"Where is your body?" Maybe I could make an anonymous phone call and set the authorities on the right path.

But Jody shrugged. "I can't remember. The last thing I recall was going out for my after-dinner stroll. And then..." He grimaced and held out his hands.

"Which way did you walk?" Maybe I could be one of those joggers who happened upon a body. Would it be too suspicious if I'd never jogged before?

Another head shake. "I can't remember. I always took a different path."

Breath exploded from my lungs, along with a sound of frustration. "You're not making this easy for me."

"I'm turning out the lights," Rue called from the

stairs.

Quickly, I deposited the romances on an adult fiction endcap and turned to Jody. The ghost knew I could see him. He'd bug me until I did what he wanted. The apparition drifted closer. All the small hairs on my arms rose as he placed a transparent hand on my shoulder.

Staring into his sallow face, I caved to the inevitable. "Fine. I'll look."

"I'll meet you out front in five." He said and then wavered out of existence.

"I didn't mean now!" I hissed. Too late, the ghost was already gone.

After blowing out a breath, I strode up the stairs to the private parlor that was the sister's television room. Hatty was seated on her plush chair and a half, while Rue was sprawled in her recliner. Mage, her orange cat, curled in her lap.

"Just in time, sweets. *Reno Masters* is coming on. They're restoring a brownstone. I can't wait to see it." Rue petted the cat, who purred as he shed all over her lap.

I hesitated at the door. "I think I'll go for a walk."

"You okay?" Hatty eyed me shrewdly.

"Just a little restless." It wasn't a lie. There would be no peace to be found until I did what Jody Haversham wanted. Ghosts could be alarmingly single-minded. Probably because they didn't have jack-shit else to do.

Hatty eyed me a moment more. "Okay. Make sure

you lock up when you get back. Turn it up, Rue. I can't hear what she's saying."

"That's because you're too stubborn to wear your hearing aid." Rue obliged though and the sound of the show's theme song blared out of the tinny speakers.

I left the Bramblewick sisters and headed back down the curving wood staircase and through the kitchen door that led to the alley between the house and the detached garage. The ghost of Jody Haversham floated by the trashcans, twirling his cane like he was playing a role in some old-timey movie.

I didn't ask any more questions. It was bad enough that I'd agreed to do him a favor. With ghosts, the more I engaged with them, the longer they lingered. But when pressed, I always tried for one reason—what if I died without discovering the fate of the child I'd borne? I would want someone to help me if they could.

We wound through the village, and past Mason's General Store, the village green, over the humped-back bridge that separated the business side of the town from the residential area. The wind had picked up and I could smell the promise of snow in the air. I blew on my hands to warm my chilled skin.

Jody Haversham's body would not be on any of the main village roads. Too much traffic. After a week, someone would have found him. I wasn't about to hightail it through the woods after sunset and fall in the same ravine he had. Instead, I decided to hunt for clues. Jody had rented the attic of a converted barn from Mrs. Otis. The widow was in her mid-seventies and lived on the far side of Mist Glen in a turn-of-the-century style farmhouse. Jody had done work for her around the place to help with the upkeep. The flood-light from her front porch dispelled the gloaming and shone through the apparition by my side.

After ascending the steps, I raised my fist and then hesitated. "How did you two get on?"

Jody drifted nearby and then bobbed up and down, a ghostly sign that he was lost in thought. "Well enough. I paid my rent on time. We weren't close, but she would ask me for help unloading groceries or taking her trash to the convenience center and I would do it. She was a good landlady."

I knocked. The sound of a dog baying an alert made me draw back. Then a sharply spoken, "Git," followed by the creaking of the door. Mrs. Otis came up to my shoulder, but her eyes were sharp gray as she looked up at me in surprise. "Emma, dear. What are you doing here at this hour?"

It was only a little after eight, but for most of the residents of Mist Glen, any time after dark was considered late.

"Sorry to bother you. But I heard about Mr. Haversham and wanted to see if you needed anything."

"You are too sweet," Mrs. Otis drawled as she opened the door wider. "Won't you come in?"

Southern hospitality had to be respected. I nodded and then crossed over the threshold, pausing to scratch her old basset hound behind the ears. "How you doing, Hank?"

"Oh, he's lazy as all get-out," Mrs. Otis shuffled down the hall to her kitchen. "I think he misses Jody. That man had a way about him when it came to the critters. He wasn't what you'd call a people person. In fact, he avoided people most days. But all the animals adored him. Can I fix you some tea, Emma?"

"Sure." I sat at the counter, on the wooden bar stool and folded my chilled hands, trying to decide the best way to phrase my request. "I was wondering if there was anything I can do for you. Maybe move Jody's stuff to storage?"

Mrs. Otis waved me off. "Oh, Deputy Harding already did that."

I frowned. "He did? When?"

"The other day. On his day off. He's such a considerate young man. Even suggested his cousin Jimmy as a new tenant. Poor dear's getting divorced. The deputy knows I depend on the income to support myself."

The kettle began to whistle, and she turned her back.

Jody's ghostly forehead crinkled. Was that because he'd been replaced so fast?

I chatted with Mrs. Otis for a few more minutes before rising and putting my mug in the sink. "It's getting late. Hatty and Rue will be looking for me."

"Thanks so much for stopping in, Emma. I'll see you on Thursday." Mrs. Otis escorted me to the door.

"What's Thursday?" Jody Haversham asked as I headed back toward the bridge.

"The Romance Readers Book Club." Unlike many

other book clubs, the romance readers did read their books. One of my favorite parts of the job was hunting for a selection for them every week and seeing how they responded. Romance readers were voracious and open-minded, not to mention tons of fun. It tickled my fancy that many of the same women who gathered for Bible study on Wednesday nights were discussing the enemies-to-lovers trope twenty-four hours later. Heated discussions of billionaires vs. vampire heroes were common. Many of them read a book a day and burned through a series every week. Lately, I'd been picking up works by independently published authors to introduce them to their next favorite author.

I'd just stepped off the bridge when a car pulled up beside me. I paused when I recognized the official vehicle with Deputy Harding behind the wheel.

"Little early for a walk of shame, isn't it Emma?"

The twinkle in his brown eyes told me he was teasing. "While I'm not exactly an authority, I'm pretty sure it doesn't qualify as a walk of shame unless you're carrying your shoes."

He chuckled. "Want a ride? It's mighty cold tonight."

He wasn't wrong. The temperature had dropped several degrees, and my hands were turning numb. "Sure."

Leaving the car to idle, the deputy exited and then escorted me around the front, holding the door open for me. He was a big man, burly in stature, and he towered over me by several inches. The buttons of his brown uniform strained over his ample chest and padded belly.

"Thanks." I held my fingers out over the heat vent and offered him a smile.

"So what are you doing out so late?" Deputy Harding asked as he pulled away, leaving the ghost standing in the road behind us.

Might as well go fishing to see if he'd tell me anything. "Visiting Mrs. Otis. She said you cleaned out Jody Haversham's apartment for her."

Art nodded. "I did. She's good friends with my Aunt Deb and I wanted to do her a solid so she could find a new tenant as soon as possible." He gave me a sideways smile.

"So you don't think Jody Haversham will come back?" I probed.

He shrugged. "Not sure. Men like him tend to drift in and out of people's lives on a whim. If he does, his stuff is in storage, and he can pay the fee to get it back."

My teeth sank into my lower lip. The assessment assumed a lot. As far as the deputy and Mrs. Otis knew, the man was only missing, and yet they were all set to erase every trace of him. While I understood the widow's need, it seemed presumptuous to dismiss the possibility of the man's return.

Even though I knew he wasn't coming back.

The car rolled to a stop in front of the dark *Pages & Potions* sign. "So, I hear there's a pretty good movie coming to the theater on Friday," Deputy Harding began. "Would you like to go with me?"

Because of Rue's coaxing, I'd expected the invitation. I was about to say no but then reconsidered. He was a nice enough man. And if I spent time with him, he might be more inclined to answer questions about the missing man who I knew to be dead. "What time?"

He blinked, as though my answer surprised him. "Seven work for you?"

Pages & Potions closed at six every night. Other than book club on Thursdays, we never stayed open late. "I'll meet you there. Thanks for the ride." I scrambled out of the car and up the steps, down through the alley, and let myself in through the kitchen door.

The ghost was waiting for me inside. "Did you learn anything from the deputy?"

I didn't want to tell him what Art had said about him. It seemed rude. Instead, I shook my head. "I'll head out early in the morning and start combing the trails you took. See if we can find you that way. Good night." I shooed him into the night and shut the door firmly in his face.

He didn't look pleased, but at least the apparition didn't reappear inside the house. Proper boundaries were essential when dealing with the deceased.

Rue pushed through the door just as I hung up my parka on the oil-rubbed bronze coat hooks. "There you are, Emma. I was just thinking a hot beverage would hit the spot. Want some cider? It's mighty cold out tonight."

I grinned and nodded. After toeing off my sneakers, I sat down at the kitchen table. Rue slid a steaming mug in front of me that smelled of cinnamon, cloves, ginger, and allspice. I took a sip, letting the delicious liquid trickle down the back of my throat. With all the hot liquid I'd consumed in the last hour, I'd have to pee several times overnight. Rue's cider was too tempting, though. She always put a shot of spiced rum in the mug.

"Isn't cider usually a fall drink?" I asked and took another sip.

"There's no rule that says you can't enjoy it in February." Rue sighed as she wrapped her hands around the earthenware mug. "Besides, I've had trouble sleeping lately, so I thought this would help me relax."

My anxiety spiked the way it always did when something seemed off with the Bramblewick sisters. "Everything all right?"

Her spidery brows drew together. "I'm not sure. I have this feeling, like we're teetering on a precipice, and one wrong step will send us careening over."

Her words made all the small hairs rise on the back of my neck. "Is it anything specific?"

She shook her head and then forced a smile. "Oh, honey, don't listen to me. I'm just a foolish old woman afraid of the dark. I'll cast a protection charm under the waning moon, and everything will be fine and dandy."

"You sure?" After all the Bramblewick sisters had

done for me, I was willing to operate on a little faith, especially when it came to Rue's intuition.

"Positive. Now go scoot on up to bed and let me clean up. Hatty will have both our heads on pikes if she finds out we had cocktail hour without her."

When she rose, I gave her an impulsive hug. She started but then hugged me back. Rue had taught me everything I knew about acceptance. She smelled of autumn spices and home. She was the kindest person, and I hated seeing her unsettled.

"The universe blessed us when you dropped into our lives," she murmured as she squeezed me tight.

"I'm the one who was blessed." I pulled away and then headed upstairs.

Between the ghost of Jody Haversham and Rue's anxiety, I tossed and turned for an hour before giving in to the inevitable. It made no sense, but nothing comforted me the way touching the rough shingled wall in my bedroom did. Reaching out into the dark, I connected with the bark. Immediate heat flooded me, chasing away the cold that had burrowed like a chigger until it seemed to radiate from my marrow.

It's all right, the house told me in that rich, masculine voice. *You're safe here. I'll protect you. I'll always protect you.*

"Who are you?" It wasn't the first time I'd asked.

The answer when it came was the same as always. *A friend.* And then music filled my head. There were no words as Glimmer Ridge hummed to me until my eyelids felt heavy and I sank into sleep.

THREE

At first light, I walked as far as I dared up the trail that wound past Mrs. Otis's house. Frozen oak leaves made the path slippery, and more than once, I stumbled on hidden roots. No sign of Jody Haversham's body, though. I paused at a scenic overlook, trying to appreciate the view but more concerned with the stitch in my side. Man, I needed to get more exercise.

"Maybe you tumbled over the side?" I huffed at the ghost. "There are a lot of deep crevasses and old mine shafts in the area. It's possible you fell into one."

"Maybe," Jody sounded doubtful. "I've been exploring these trails for years. I was sure I knew where all the pitfalls were."

"I need to head back to the store. The kindergarten class is coming in for story hour at eleven." I told him.

It was an excuse. Though the morning was warm, it was still February in the mountains. Between the poor visibility and my utter lack of direction, I doubted I would ever find Jody Haversham's body. At least not by myself.

"Maybe I can get Deputy Harding to help," I suggested as we headed back down the trail toward the village. "I can hint around that you wouldn't just pack up and leave. That he should be looking for you. The sheriff's office has a ton more resources than I do."

"Do you really think they'd care?" Jody's tone was sullen. "They packed up all my stuff over the weekend."

I wanted to put a hand on his shoulder in comfort. But though I could hear and see the dead, I couldn't touch them.

The kitchen smelled of oatmeal raisin cookies when I walked in. Rue was wearing one of her ankle-length floral dresses and her glasses were perched on top of her head as she checked on her baking.

"Hatty's looking for you," Rue informed me as I hung up my coat.

I'd been about to head upstairs to shower but paused. "Do you know why?"

She shook her head. "No, but she's like a weasel with a sore tooth, so watch yourself."

Fantastic. I ran a hand through my windblown hair and then pushed through the kitchen door into the bookshop.

"Where were you?" Hatty snapped as she glanced up from her laptop.

"I went for a walk."

"Alone?"

Do tagalongs count? I wondered as Jody Haversham drifted into the local legends section. "Yeah. Is something wrong?"

Hatty rubbed her chest. Her steel gray brows were pulled tightly together. "I had a bad dream. About you. When I got up to check on you, you were gone."

I moved behind the counter and poured a cup of coffee, then slid it across the counter to her. "I'm sorry, Hatty. I didn't mean to worry you. Next time, I'll leave a note."

"Why didn't you tell me you went to Mrs. Otis's last night?"

I frowned. "How do you know about that?"

"Deputy Harding stopped by this morning. Said he gave you a ride last night, and that you dropped a glove in his car. What's going on with you, Emma?" She handed me the glove I hadn't even been aware I'd had with me.

"Nothing." The lie scalded my throat as I took the glove from her. I never kept secrets from Hatty and Rue. But I knew how they felt about my mixing in with the deceased. How else was I supposed to deal with the tagalong situation? It was easy for Hatty to tell me to ignore them. But since she couldn't see or hear the apparitions, she didn't know how insistent they could be.

Perhaps I should tell her what I was doing. A clever woman who knew Mist Glen better than me might have some idea how to locate Jody Haversham's body.

I opened my mouth to confess when the little bell above the front door jangled and the kindergarten class poured in.

"Sorry, I know we're a little early," Ms. Bedford, the new kindergarten teacher at Mist Glen Elementary, gave us a harried smile. She was a pretty woman in her mid-thirties with blue eyes, apple cheeks, and a bleached blonde bob that didn't match her dark eyebrows at all. Her Yankee accent was thick as she added, "The heat's broken in my classroom this morning and we needed to clear out so maintenance could work on it."

"It's fine." Hatty shut her laptop and then took it and her coffee back to her bedroom as the noise in the bookstore grew to a dull roar.

I helped shepherd the five- and six-year-olds into the children's room while Ms. Bedford dealt with removing coats, bathroom trips, story requests, and reminding them of the rules of participating in story hour.

"It's like herding cats," she grumbled as she made yet another trip to the bathroom with a little girl in pink overalls.

I grinned and got busy handing out wooden cars to several of the students who wanted to drive on the road rug in the far corner. Some of the kids needed to burn a little steam before they could settle down enough to listen to a book. What would the child I'd given birth to be like? Loud like the boy in the denim overalls who was singing *The Wheels on the Bus* at the top of his lungs? Or maybe shy like the girl with the pink sweater and corduroys who pretended to read a story to a stuffed giraffe?

Rue bustled in with snacks and helped line up the class for a squirt of hand sanitizer. We served juice boxes and apple slices as Ms. Bedford selected the story, *The Velveteen Rabbit*.

"This one always makes me cry," she confessed as she offered me the book. "Will you read it, please, Emma?"

I agreed. Though public speaking wasn't my jam, when it came to telling tales, I loved to be the center of the children's universe, if only for a little while. Sitting on the low curved bench, I leaned my back against the rough-hewn wall. Glimmer Ridge didn't speak to me, but I could feel that same presence as I began the story about a child who loved his inanimate toy so much that it became real.

"I'm beat," Rue sighed an hour later as the line of students disappeared around the bend toward the elementary school. "I have no idea how Sissy deals with them all day, every day."

"Sissy?" I asked with a frown.

"Sissy Bedford. The new teacher." Rue patted my arm. "She might be a nice friend for you."

"Another setup?" Hatty emerged from her office. "Can't you just leave Emma be?"

"It's not a setup to encourage her to make friends," Rue huffed. "Not everyone is a cranky lone wolf like you."

Hatty glared, and I turned my back before she spied my smile. I headed into the children's room and began picking up the trash and returning the cars to the bin.

Jody Haversham appeared beside me. "I remembered something."

I let out a tired breath. "What?"

"The night I went missing? I got a phone call from my sister."

"Okay," I hedged.

"Whenever I argued with my sister, I liked to walk the old quarry up behind the railroad tracks."

"You're sure you argued with her?" I asked while straightening the cushions.

His countenance grew darker. "We always argue. She didn't like the things I said on my podcast."

I had no idea he had a podcast. Much like everyone else in Mist Glen, I was getting the impression that if I couldn't see ghosts, I wouldn't have noticed his disappearance either.

"What was the podcast called?" My phone was in the front room, but I would check it out as soon as I got the chance.

"*The Witching Hour*. It's a history of occult legends and oddities in Appalachia. Especially witchcraft."

I blinked. "Witchcraft?"

"I wasn't into devil worship or anything like that." The ghost grew defensive. "That's what Melany thought. She's very religious and after every episode, she'd call me to rant and rave about how I would burn in hell for the things I said. My research was sacrilegious. It embarrassed her. I always embarrassed her and our mother."

I swallowed. "So the quarry?" It was an isolated place, several miles from the village. If he'd had an accident or perhaps a heart attack out there, it was no wonder no one had unearthed his body.

The ghost nodded. "I wouldn't suggest you go alone."

"I wasn't planning on it." After the struggle I had with such an easy hike that morning, the challenge of the quarry trail was too much for me to handle. Maybe I could make an anonymous phone call to the police. Better yet, get someone else to report it.

"Where does your sister live?" I asked.

"Over in Pine Hill." He named a town about twenty miles to the east of Mist Glen. I knew the area. It was where Hatty and Rue met with their coven for full moon and Sabbat gatherings.

"If I can get your sister to report you as missing and tell the sheriff where you used to walk, maybe we can find you." I just needed to come up with a good reason to take the truck to Pine Hill.

Rue gave me the perfect excuse at dinner. "A date with the deputy!" She clapped her hands like a small child and beamed at me. "What are you going to wear?"

"Um, I hadn't thought about it." Not a lie. Between the ghost, my search for his body, and story hour, I didn't have room in my head to think about the date that wasn't a date.

"Maybe I can go to the outlet mall over near Pine Hill tomorrow," I spoke in a casual tone. "You know Thursdays are slow until the Romance Book Club comes in. Would it be all right if I took the truck?"

"Make sure you fill it up with gas on the way back. What have you got for the club this week?" Hatty asked as she cut into her meatloaf.

"Paranormal women's fiction romance." I chatted about my latest find, the Silver Sisters series, which I thought would be a great hit with our club members. "You ladies would love it, full of witchy goodness."

Hatty snorted. "Most authors never get witches right. They're either evil old crones or sexy succubus or incubus types."

My fork fell numbly from my fingers.

"Emma?" Rue put a hand on my arm. "Is everything okay?"

My heart pounded, and my palms sweated. There was no reason for the visceral reaction, yet I couldn't stop it.

"Emma?" Hatty's tone broke me from the odd trance.

"Sorry." I forced a smile and picked up my fork.

"What's going on with you lately?" Hatty's gaze narrowed on me.

"Nothing. I just got a weird feeling." Done with dinner, I rose and collected the plates. After washing the dishes, I located my set of earbuds from under the counter in the front room and hunted for *The Witching Hour* podcast. Selecting an episode at random, I listened to Jody Haversham's familiar voice while I dusted and straightened the store.

After three episodes, I felt sure Hatty and Rue would appreciate the amount of research Jody put into understanding witchcraft. He talked about rituals and Sabbats, and the phases of the moon, as well as where some of the more bizarre legends came from. The whole broom-riding thing? It was naked people absorbing hallucinogenic compounds through their nether regions. Jody had a dry wit and painted a vivid picture with words. I had to hand it to the dead man— he had done his homework.

"Many believe that the Salem Witch trials were the only incidents of witch persecution in North America. Nothing could be further from the truth. While the witch trials in Massachusetts were well documented, many others were never spoken of outside of the settlements where they happened. In the mountains of North Carolina alone, several unmarked graves have been discovered. Typically, the bodies fit the descriptions of those accused of witchcraft, women in their forties and up, and those who defended them. Based on the tales out of Europe, we can speculate that these women also had a basic understanding of herbs and healing. Many of them lived on the outskirts of civilization. A perfect scapegoat to blame when things went wrong.

"Society threw them away after blaming all their problems on them. Women and men suspected of witchcraft had

a habit of disappearing under mysterious circumstances, which continues to this day."

A shiver stole over me. The same had happened to Jody. And maybe to me.

Unsettled, I headed back upstairs to take a shower. I spent longer than usual under the tepid spray, trying to let my thoughts coalesce. While I'd only listened to a few episodes, I didn't get what had gotten Jody's sister's skivvies in a twist over the podcast. It wasn't like her brother was advocating for witches. He'd described what had happened to witches in the region.

While slowly running a comb through my hair, I stood by the window and stared at the silver moon behind the tall pines in the direction of the quarry. If Jody had been around, I would have asked the ghost what it was about that desolate space that compelled him to go there to brood.

I lay down in bed and of its own volition, my hand drifted to the wood shingled wall.

You're safe, Glimmer Ridge told me.

"What are you?" I whispered to the voice.

Would you read to me? The voice asked instead.

I blinked. "What would you like to hear?"

It doesn't matter. I just want to listen to your voice.

I swallowed. It was the first time Glimmer Ridge had asked anything of me. After all the reassurance the house had given me, how could I refuse? Slowly, I reached over to my nightstand and cracked the spine of my latest book. I could feel the house

47

settling around me and soon I replaced my worries with tales of a mythical knight questing for his true love.

I took the truck out early and drove the twenty-two miles to Pine Hill, where Melany Haversham-Keats lived. The ghost was riding shotgun. If I didn't know better, I would have thought Jody was nervous to see his sister.

"How long has it been?" I asked as we took the turn onto Birch Street. "Since you've seen her, I mean?"

"About seven years."

I let out a slow breath. It was none of my business and I shouldn't get in any deeper. My job was straightforward. Get Melany to call the sheriff and report her brother missing. Mention that he liked to hike by the quarry. The freaking end.

Stay out of it, Emma. The voice of reason in my head sounded suspiciously like Hatty.

Jody directed me up a gravel drive to a brick ranch-style house. The windows were old but clean, and the porch swept. A tire swing hung from the naked branch of a maple in the center of the dormant yard. Very middle America.

I pulled to a stop and glanced over at the house.

"You don't have to come in if you don't want to," I told the ghost.

He gave me a tight smile. "It's not like Melany was shy about her opinions when I was alive. I knew what she thought of me and what I did in my spare time. Besides, she can't hurt me now."

I wasn't so sure, but it was his choice. The gravel crunched beneath my boots as I circled the truck and then headed up the three stairs to the front door. A plump woman in her late fifties wearing a green ankle-length dress and low-heeled pumps answered the door. "Can I help you?"

"Hi. My name is Emma and I'm friends with your brother's landlady. I was in town on an errand and was wondering if you have seen or heard from Jody lately?"

Her expression of curiosity morphed into suspicion. "No."

My forced smile wobbled at her curt tone. "It's just that she's going to have to rent his apartment to somebody else if we can't find him. Did he happen to mention where he was going the last time you spoke to him?"

"No, if you'll excuse me..." She tried to shut the door, but I wedged my boot in the jam so she couldn't slam it in my face.

"Please," I breathed, trying to strike a balance between concerned citizen and pushy stalker. "I'm afraid something bad has happened to him. If you could just call the sheriff's office and report—"

She didn't let me get it all out before interrupting. "If something did happen to my brother, it's no surprise to me. Jody was reckless, and he refused to heed my warnings."

"Warnings about what?" I asked. "Did someone threaten him? Or you?"

Her gaze darted around. "You need to leave, now."

"Are you afraid of someone?" I don't know where my persistence came from, but I couldn't let it go. "Please, I'm just trying to help your brother."

She blew out an exasperated breath. "You want to know about my brother? Ask his wife."

Her words hit me like a shove. I took an involuntary step back, and she slammed the door in my face.

FOUR

"Lucy, you've got some 'splaining to do." I singsonged to the ghost in the truck. Using the old television punchline hid my exasperation.

"What did she say?" Jody Haversham asked.

"Um, that you have a wife." Irritated, I yanked my seatbelt hard, and the stupid thing got stuck. "Why didn't you mention her?"

The ghost wavered and then vanished.

"Oh, come on!" My voice echoed off the walls of the empty truck. "You're the one who dragged me into this and now you're being evasive? The hell!"

No one answered. I had two choices—either I could sit in the truck and rant like a lunatic, or I could go buy the dress I'd told the Bramblewick sisters I'd come to Pine Hill for and add a partial truth to my sojourn.

"Fricking ghosts," I muttered and threw the

vehicle into drive. Hatty was right. This so-called "gift" of mine was nothing but a pain in the ass. There was no helping the dead. They were dead. Either someone would find Jody Haversham's body, or they wouldn't. It had nothing to do with me. Nothing I did would bring him back to life. I needed to mind my own business, keep my nose clean, and let the dead sort themselves out.

An icy rain began to ping off the truck as I pulled into the massive parking area for the outlet mall. I selected a store at random and pulled up my hood. Maybe other women enjoyed trying on clothes in public spaces. I'd never seen the appeal. Why bother going out when you could order online? Gas to the nearest store costs more than shipping from most places.

Whatever, I'd made the trip and though I was in no mood for it, I might as well buy the quintessential LBD and be done with it.

Three stores in, I found what I was looking for. It wasn't a little black dress, but a dark blue one. It had a sweetheart neckline that worked wonders on my cleavage and a U shape at the back that exposed a lot of skin. Though the hemline was shorter than I liked, it was flattering to my heavyset thighs. The dress seemed a little fancy for a movie date, but it looked so good there was no way I could leave it behind.

After forking over my credit card to a twenty-something with an eyebrow piercing and a bored expression, I signed for the dress and carried my purchase out to the truck.

The ghost was waiting for me in the cab of the truck.

"Let me explain," the apparition began as I climbed in.

I carefully draped my dress through him and over the seat. "No need."

"Emma—"

"Oh no," I said to him as I shook ice pellets off my coat. "I am done with you for the day, you hear me? D-O-N-E, done."

Funny thing about death, it didn't stop people from being liars. I'd wasted the last two days getting tangled up in his mess. I had a good life with Hatty and Rue. Helping the dead would only screw that up. If I was going to help anyone, I should start with myself and try to get my memories back. Unlike Jody Haversham, I had a life that could be fixed.

Resolve firmly mounted to the sticking place, I ignored the ghost's attempts at conversation and clicked on the radio. Eventually, he got the hint and retreated to wherever he went when he wasn't with me.

Two miles from the village, the skies opened, the snow coming down until I could barely see the hood of the truck out the windshield. The hills grew more treacherous as I approached Mist Glen. I slowed to a crawl. At least no one else appeared to be out—

A man appeared in the middle of the road.

I gasped. Tried to slam on the brakes.

The pedal went all the way to the floor. No resistance as the truck careened forward. Desperate, I spun the wheel.

The back end of the truck fishtailed. It wasn't until the truck sailed through his body that I realized the being on the road was Jody Haversham's ghost.

Well, this is a stupid way to die.

Sliding sideways, the truck skidded until the passenger's side door connected with a massive pine. The airbag exploded into my face. The impact stole my awareness.

I awoke to the taste of blood and the sound of a frantic male voice. "Emma, Emma, are you hurt? I'm so sorry."

Blinking slowly, I saw the fuzzy outline of the ghost that had caused me to wreck Hatty's truck.

"I'll get help." Jody patted the air between us.

How? I was the only one who could see him. I wanted to ask but was too sore to pose a question.

It must have occurred to him too, since he spun in a slow circle. "Emma—,"

"Leave me alone," I whispered.

He froze, and then, with a look of horror on his face, he vanished.

Though I wanted nothing more than to shut my eyes, I knew I couldn't stay in the truck. There might be a gas leak or something else that would catch the vehicle on fire.

I took a moment to inventory my body. Though I

felt sore all over and had bitten my tongue badly, nothing appeared to be broken or bleeding.

Slowly, I reached for the seatbelt and pressed the button to unhook it. It clicked free. Then I had to fight the airbag down to get the stupid thing to deflate enough to give me room to maneuver.

I fumbled with the door handle until it popped. My whole body shook as I tumbled from the truck onto the icy road. More pain wracked me. The heavy, wet snow picked up as I slowly limped away from the vehicle, shivering from shock and cold.

Phone. Where was my phone? My purse had been lodged between the crumpled passenger's side wheel well, but after checking my pockets, my numb hands found the phone in my jacket pocket. At least one thing was working in my favor.

I had just begun to dial *Pages & Potions* when a battered Honda Civic turned the corner. Through the swiftly moving wipers, I saw the shocked face of Sissy Bedford, Mist Glen's new kindergarten teacher.

She pulled up beside me and threw open the door, making a beeline for me. "Emma! Are you okay? What happened?"

"I crashed."

"I can see that." Her tone was dry. "Are you hurt?"

"Just bruised, I think. Could you give me a ride?"

"Of course." Offering her arm, she helped me to her car, holding open the door. I grunted as I sat, the bruises singing in protest. I wanted nothing more than to curl up in my bed for the next week.

"Are you sure I shouldn't take you to the hospital?" she asked. "You might have internal bleeding."

I cracked an eyelid at her. "To be honest, I want to get off these roads as soon as possible. Doc Trammel can always come to check on me."

She cast me a worried glance but thankfully, headed into the village, toward *Pages & Potions*.

"About time, girl, I was getting—" Hatty's words cut off as she got a good look at my pathetic figure limping into the bookstore. "My word, what happened?"

"Skidded on some ice." The pain in my ribs and the trouble I had breathing told me that something wasn't right. "Truck might be totaled. Sorry."

"Oh, honey," Hatty smoothed some hair off my face. "Don't worry about that."

"We should report the accident," Sissy murmured.

"Rue!" Hatty bellowed. "Call Doc. Emma's been hurt."

Rue pushed through the kitchen door, took one look at me, and gasped. She fumbled in her apron, most likely looking for her glasses and phone. I hated to see her so flustered. Hatty either. It reminded me of the night I'd first appeared on their doorstep, weak and bleeding and in desperate need of help.

That was my last thought before the bookstore started to spin. "I don't feel so well," I whispered.

"She's going to pass out!" Sissy cried.

The world around me tunneled, and I faded away.

MIST SURROUNDED ME, obscuring the landscape, though I could smell the salty tang of ocean air and hear the roar from the ocean. Beneath my heavy tread boots, I spied golden sand.

And I wasn't alone.

The presence from Glimmer Ridge had followed me.

"What happened?" His tone was sharp, nothing like the crooning loverlike tone that put me at ease.

"How did you know?" I rounded toward the voice, hoping to catch a glimpse of him. My eyes scanned the haze and found nothing.

"I'm connected to you, Emma. I can feel your fear. Your pain." The mist rose and caressed my cheek.

My lids drifted shut and the hand on my face grew more solid. "Why?"

"I asked you first."

A shuddering breath escaped my lungs. Somehow, the pain had followed me into this odd dreamscape. No one else would believe what had happened with Jody Haversham. I needed to unload. My dream guy wasn't about to spread my secrets around. "A ghost that I've been trying to help. He pissed me off, and I was ignoring him." My brow crinkled as I thought the situation through. "I think he appeared in the middle of the road to try to get my attention. I didn't realize who it was until I lost control of the truck. But then when I tried to stop, the brakes didn't work."

"You could have been killed," that rich voice growled. "I hope you banished the ghost."

"Banished?" I frowned. "What are you talking about?"

He hesitated. Desperate for answers I reached up and gripped the hand that caressed me. "Please, tell me what you know."

"I shouldn't interfere," he muttered. "This is your journey of discovery."

I licked suddenly dry lips. "Please, if you know something about me, anything that will help me remember my life from before, I need to know."

He sighed. I felt what I thought was his forehead pressing into mine. "All right, my love, but this needs to stay between us. I didn't want you to find out this way but, you can command the dead."

It took every ounce of willpower not to lift my lids and stare. "I can?"

"I've seen you do it. The other day out in front of the house. You made that apparition leave his wife alone. They must do what you say."

"Why?" I whispered. "What am I?"

A pause. Lips trailed over my cheekbone in a light caress before he whispered, "You are unique in this world. One who has seen beyond the veil. You, Emma, are a true mystic."

"A mystic?" I shook my head. "Is that like a medium?"

"A medium can only commune with the ghosts. You can dispatch them like they are soldiers and you are their commanding officer." The hand on my face fell away. "You've been here too long. You must return to your body, or it will not fully heal."

"Wait!" I called out, desperate for more information. But I sensed he'd left.

"Damn," I snarled. I'd learned nothing about him, not even his name. But at least he had given me a word for what I was—a mystic.

Opening my eyes, I found myself on the floor of *Pages & Potions*. The ice in my hair had melted, leaving the silver brown tresses in a wet snarl. Doc Trammel stood over me, appearing relieved that my eyes were open. "There's the girl. How're you feeling, Emma?"

"Like I ran into a tree." In the dream, my mystery man called me a mystic. What was that? Was he real or just some random byproduct of my imagination? I had been reading a ton of supernatural books lately.

"Can you walk?" Hatty asked.

I nodded, then winced.

"I think we should take her to the hospital," Doc said gruffly. "She may have internal bleeding."

Rue squeaked, "Oh Emma, that doesn't sound good."

"I'll be fine." I tried to reassure her, but the anxious way she wrung her hands made me cave. "If it will make you feel better, Rue, I'll go to the hospital though I don't think it's necessary."

"What about the store?" Sissy asked.

"We'll close up," Hatty decided. "No one is coming out in this cursed weather anyhow."

Doc Trammel drove us to the county hospital, where I sat in one of those dehumanizing threadbare gowns and waited for an age. Hatty sent out an email blast from her phone that the romance book club meeting was canceled, which depressed my spirits further.

It was fully dark by the time we returned to Glimmer Ridge. I had cracked several ribs when the airbag deployed, which accounted for the struggle every time I tried to take a full breath. Other than some bruising, though, I was pronounced fit to return home if I promised to take it easy.

"I'm so sorry about the truck," I told the Bramblewicks as they helped me up the stairs to my bedroom.

"Pish, I was ready to trade it in anyhow," Hatty grunted. Maybe it was all in my mind, but she seemed to have as much trouble catching her breath as I did. "We'll go shopping with the insurance check."

I forced a smile, even as guilt flayed me. I knew what their financial situation looked like. There was a reason Hatty spent a good chunk of her days working the books and trying to make every penny stretch. If not for paying me a salary, the sisters would live comfortably. But they insisted on a wage as well as giving me room and board. Their kindness stretched their finances thin. Add my new medical bills and the cost of a new vehicle to the mix and we might be in some serious trouble.

Maybe I should look for part-time work. The only problem was, I was unskilled labor. And picking up another full-time job might only make a dent.

Plus, there were my...issues. No social security number, at least not one I'd been born with. An employment history that consisted of making coffee, dusting, and reading. Never mind that Mist Glen wasn't exactly bustling with economic opportunities.

"Stop thinking," Hatty snapped as we paused outside my room.

"How did you know?" I asked.

"I could smell something burning."

I scoffed and then grimaced. "Ow."

"Let's get you to bed," Rue clucked like a mother hen.

I looked over at the sisters. Their faces appeared lined, almost haggard.

"It's okay. I can take it from here."

"Are you sure, Emma?" Rue was back to hand wringing.

"Positive. Good night." I slipped into the bathroom, leaving them no choice but to disperse.

Sitting down to pee was rough. The thought of getting back up made me whimper. Though I felt grubby, I thought the shower was asking too much. Instead, I did my best to clean off the grime on my face with a washcloth. Exhaustion swamped me by the time I hobbled across the hall to my bedroom, so it took me a moment to understand what I was seeing.

On the bed was my purse. And beside it, someone had carefully laid out the blue dress.

I f I had any dreams that night, they vanished with the rising sun. When I limped back into the bathroom, the sight of my reflection, all swelling and ugly bruises, made my insides lurch. The date with Deputy Harding was imminent. I hoped the man had a strong stomach.

It took me a long time to shower, longer still, to make my way down the stairs into the bookshop and over to the coffee pot. No sign of Hatty yet, but I could hear Rue puttering around the kitchen, baking up what smelled like apple streusel muffins.

Hatty appeared and grimaced when she caught sight of my face. "It's a good thing you and the deputy are going to a movie where it's nice and dark."

Hatty never blew smoke.

"Oh, hush you." Rue scurried forward with a tray full of muffins and arranged them in the glass pastry case we kept on the counter. "It's not all about looks, you know."

"And thank the stars for it," Hatty grumbled as she poured herself a mug of coffee. "Emma, sit down before you fall down."

"It's better when I'm standing," I told her.

"Maybe you should reschedule." Rue worried her bottom lip. "I'm sure the deputy would understand."

Tempting though that thought was, I promised to help the ghost of Jody Haversham. He must have been the one to return the dress and my purse to my room. I assumed it was an apology for causing the wreck. "I'll be okay. I was thinking of emailing the recommended book list to the Romance Book Club and then working on the newsletter. Anything special we want to add?"

The three of us had an impromptu meeting to talk shop. Our newsletter was bi-monthly. We advertised sales and events at the store. Rue always included a recipe while Hatty offered up her favorite reads of the month. I tried to include fun bits like character interviews and fake date-with-a-book boyfriend quizzes. Indie authors were so creative with their marketing.

The ice from the day before had melted by noon and residents of Mist Glen came into *Pages & Potions* to gawk at my multicolored visage. I answered numerous questions about the accident and took sympathy from everyone who "poor Emma-ed" me. By far, my favorite visit was from Sissy.

"You look like shit," the kindergarten teacher told me.

I laughed and immediately regretted it as pain lanced through my face.

She winced. "Sorry."

"You teach kindergarten. You shouldn't say shit."

She blew air between her lips. "Says who? It's not like I say it in class. Besides, everyone needs a vice."

"True that," Hatty piped up. "Do me a solid and help Emma find one."

I rolled my eyes. "Ignore her."

"So," Sissy followed me to the mystery section where I was unboxing the latest shipment. "I hear you're dating Deputy Harding."

My jaw dropped. "Who told you that?"

"The janitor at school. The woman at the grocery store, and most recently, Rue."

I sighed. "We haven't even been out yet. I swear, if it was up to Mist Glen, they'd have a date circled on the calendar for our wedding."

Sissy shrugged. "It's a small community. Do you like him?"

I hedged by saying, "He's a nice enough man."

"Well, there's a ringing endorsement." Sissy grimaced and then asked, "Who was your teenage celebrity crush?"

"I can't remember. It was so long ago..." Hatty was wrong, I couldn't afford a vice. Between my shadowed past and the ghost thing, I was keeping way too many secrets.

"So that guy that disappeared?" Sissy changed the subject, jerking me to a halt with a book in my hand.

"What about him?"

"Did you know he hosted this kick-ass podcast about the occult in the Carolinas?"

I laughed. "Funny you mention it, since I just started listening the other day."

She shook her bleach-blonde head. "I wonder if his whole disappearing act was just to boost his ratings."

"Nah, Jody wasn't like that." The second the words were out, I wished I could summon them back.

"Jody?" Her eyes went wide. "So you knew him?"

"Everyone knows everyone else in Mist Glen." I dodged. "He used to come

in here sometimes." With all the tap dancing I was doing around the truth, I was going to be in terrific shape by the time they found his body.

Sissy seemed to accept that. "It's odd the things you don't know about people you see every day, you know? Of course, I have the best inside source in the world. Nothing like a five-year-old to spill all the dirty details. And the best part is they don't even know they're doing it."

We both laughed.

Sissy headed out and I stepped behind the counter to pour coffee and serve more of Rue's muffins. By the time Hatty flipped the sign to closed, I was ready to collapse.

Of course, that was when Deputy Art Harding rapped on the door. He wore jeans, a denim shirt, cowboy boots, a sherpa-lined corduroy coat, and a black ten-gallon hat, looking every bit the part of the well-fed country boy.

"Emma," he said, his brows drawing together in concern. "I just heard about the accident. Are you all right?"

"It looks worse than it is," I told him. "But I understand if you don't want to be seen with me."

"It would take more than a few bruises to hide your beauty." His tone was admiring.

Heat scalded my face. I fervently hoped the date wasn't going to give him the wrong impression.

"Just give me a few minutes to get changed."

"Take your time. I know I'm early. I thought maybe we'd stop by Lou's taco truck on the way."

Be still my heart. Tacos—not just for Tuesdays anymore. "Sounds great."

I picked my way carefully upstairs. No amount of makeup would disguise the mess the airbag had made of my face. It wasn't like the entire population of Mist Glen hadn't already figured out what was up.

I brushed my teeth and my hair, deciding to leave it down, and then headed into my room. The blue dress hung from the back of the closet door. My teeth sank into my lower lip. I hadn't lied to Sissy when I told her Deputy Harding was a nice man. He was. But in my weirdness, I preferred the vision of the ghost of Glimmer Ridge. Who I couldn't see. And might be nothing more than a hallucination.

That dress meant business. Wearing it on a date

was like saying, *I like you enough to show some skin and will tempt you to touch it.*

And I couldn't go there. Not yet. Maybe never.

I'd had sex at least once and had the scar to prove it. The thought of getting naked and busy with a man unsettled me to my core. Hell, that was probably why I'd conjured an image of a protector that had no corporeal body. Like a genie in a bottle that occasionally gave me answers. When it came to Art Harding, though, I didn't want to plant false hope. He deserved better than my neurotic self, especially when I was half in love with the spirit of Glimmer Ridge.

"He's not...real, Emma." Time to choose clothing that said 'casual and friendly.' I reached for a light gray sweater that wasn't too tatty. I paired it with a long broomstick skirt, calf-high boots with a low heel and the amethyst necklace Hatty had given me on the first anniversary of my showing up at the store. It was the day I always thought of as my child's birthday.

After heading back down the stairs, I wasn't at all surprised to see Rue offering the deputy a mug. She turned and her expression fell when she saw what I was wearing. She didn't comment on it. Instead, she forced a smile and murmured, "I hope you two have fun."

Deputy Harding held my coat and then offered me an arm as he led me down the stairs to the freshly salted sidewalk and then over to his car.

The taco truck was usually parked in the hardware store parking lot, so we headed in that direction. He made small talk about the weather, which was fine by me. I had a daily limit on talking and I'd about reached my quota.

"Where were you before you came to Mist Glen?" he asked suddenly.

Crap. I fumbled for the background story that Hatty had come up with five years before. "Memphis, why?"

He shrugged. "No one knew for sure. What made you come here?"

And this is why I don't date. "It's complicated," I hedged. Even if he was off duty, I didn't feel great fibbing to an officer of the law.

"You can just tell me it's none of my business if I'm being too nosy." he laughed. "Afraid it's a habit formed on the job."

"And that will work?" I quirked a brow.

He shrugged. "Well, I'll still be curious, but I won't pry. I'd rather you open up to me when you're ready, Emma."

My smile was tight. That would probably never happen. Better to obfuscate.

"I got out of a bad relationship," Not a lie. It couldn't have been great, not the way I'd shown up on Hatty and Rue's doorstep. No decent man would have left the mother of his child in that condition. I made a conscious effort not to think of the baby's father and the role he must have played in what happened.

The line for the food truck inched forward, and I shivered.

"Cold?" Art Harding asked.

"I'm fine." I focused on him so as not to fixate on the apparition across the street. Jody Haversham kept his distance at least. Just like I'd ordered him to. Could I really command the ghosts?

It wasn't the time to experiment. Or to think about my dream.

Instead, I focused on getting the answers I needed to help the ghost find peace. "Did you know that Jody Haversham had a podcast?"

"Oh, yeah?" He sounded disinterested. Didn't look at me as the line surged again. He placed his order, and I placed mine. One bean burrito, one cheese quesadilla smothered with fried onions. If that didn't send a friends-only vibe, I didn't know what would. Once we were given our food, we headed back to the car to eat.

I waited until we were seated with the heater blasting before bringing up the topic again. "Yeah. I was listening to it the other day."

Art Harding blinked at me. "Listening to what?"

"The podcast." Was he even listening to me? "It dawned on me that the content was the sort that might get people riled up."

He held up both his hands. "Hang on a minute there, Emma. What are you suggesting?"

Appetite gone, I tore parts of my burrito wrapper into bits. "Nothing. I just don't like how easy it seems for this town to forget that Jody Haversham was part of it."

His warm hand covered mine. When I glanced up,

his warm brown eyes were fixed on mine. "Look, if you want, I'll make a few phone calls. Rattle a few cages. Would that make you feel better?"

"Yes," I breathed. "It would."

"You're good people, Emma." He squeezed my hand once. "Now eat your burrito."

I did, feeling lighter than I had since the night the ghost of Jody Haversham appeared in *Pages & Potions*.

"How was it?" Rue pounced on me the second I let myself in through the back door.

"Fairly predictable," I muttered as I hung up my coat. "But you know what they say—you've seen one action flick, you've seen them all."

"Not the movie, the date." Rue set the kettle on the burner. "Did the two of you click?"

"Leave her alone, Rue." Hatty groused from behind her computer screen.

"Sorry, Rue. I'm just not that into him." I smiled to soften the blow. "He's a very nice man and I wish him well, but we aren't a love match." There was no one thing about the deputy that I could point to and say that's why—other than he wasn't my dream guy.

Rue's face fell. "Oh. Well, maybe if you get to know each other better...?"

I shook my head. It had been awkward enough

escaping into the house tonight. Art Harding was the kind of guy who thought no meant ask again later. He said he respected me for "playing hard to get". I hadn't been playing. "Not interested, Rue."

"I just want you to be happy, Emma."

"I am." Usually. When I wasn't having a panic attack or being inundated with requests from the other side. "I'm going to bed. Good night, ladies."

"Night." Hatty winked as I escaped to the stairs.

Exhausted, I headed into my room and felt relief when I pressed my forehead to the door. "That was a terrible idea."

"Yes," Glimmer Ridge agreed.

I scowled, though I kept my hand on the door. "Then why didn't you stop me?"

"You need to live your life on your terms." In my mind's eye, I pictured invisible shoulders shrugging.

"I guess we're not going steady then," I grumbled. What did I expect? For the incorporeal house spirit to be jealous? Unlikely. He was a house and probably a figment of my damaged mind. I let my hand fall away and grabbed my phone.

I'd intended to listen to more of Jody's podcast but instead found myself searching for the definition of a mystic.

The search results were mixed—Mystic, Connecticut, *Mystic Pizza*, the movie. I kept scrolling until I came to the spiritual definition. *A person who is connected to the divine.* More religious texts talked about the devout people who straddled the line between our world and the one beyond, often called the astral plane.

I found nothing about communicating with ghosts. Or ordering them around. More evidence I was looney.

I took my time changing into my warmest pajamas, then padded barefoot across the hall to brush my teeth. At least one thing had gone well. Deputy Harding had agreed to look for Jody Haversham. That officially let me off the hook as the primary searcher.

Letting out a sigh, I collapsed back onto the bed, making sure not to make direct contact with Glimmer Ridge. What I needed now was a decent night's sleep, no more weird communication, or hot lust-filled dreams.

The pounding on my bedroom door pulled me from sleep. A glance toward the window told me it was still dark. Blinking, I murmured, "Come in,"

"Emma dear," Rue, swaddled in her tattered floral bathrobe, her silver hair up in curlers, stood at my door. "Deputy Harding is here to see you."

"Now?" My brows pulled together. "About what?"

"He won't say, but he's insisting." Rue's teeth sank into her bottom lip. "Hatty tried to put him off until later, but he wasn't having it."

"Okay." I tossed the covers back and then grabbed a pair of thick socks. Tugging them on would prevent me from making direct contact with Glimmer Ridge. I could feel the house's anxiety and didn't need the distraction. There could only be one reason why

Deputy Harding had shown up long before the store opened. He must have found something about Jody Haversham.

Heart pounding, I made my way down the stairs. Hatty and Art Harding waited at the bottom. He wore his uniform, though his hat was in his big hands. As a floorboard creaked under my weight, two sets of eyes turned to face me.

"Emma," Deputy Harding's twang grew thicker as he said, "I need you to come with me."

"Now?" Hatty's tone was incredulous.

"Am I under arrest?" I asked.

He shook his head. "Not officially but the sheriff wants to talk to you."

"About what?" Hatty snapped.

Deputy Harding didn't hold my gaze as he spoke the words that chilled me to the bone. "The murder of Jody Haversham."

SIX

T hankfully, Art Harding didn't handcuff me. He let me put on my jacket and sneakers and then guided me down to the patrol car. Unlike the other night when he'd given me a ride, he did urge me into the backseat. Hatty followed us outside, demanding answers the deputy didn't give.

My heart pounded, and I felt dizzy. My stomach lurched as the dinner I hadn't fully digested threatened to make a reappearance. *Don't throw up,* I told myself. Regurgitation wouldn't help.

"Murdered," I whispered. Never in a million years would it have occurred to me that someone had killed Jody Haversham. No wonder his ghost had been so insistent about being found. Sure, I'd alluded to someone maybe having a grudge against him because of the podcast and his sister had been acting weird, but still. I hadn't thought my ruse would end up with me in the back of a patrol car. What were the odds that —I checked the time on the dashboard—less than ten hours after the end of our date, Art would have not only found Jody but confirmed that the man had been murdered?

Deputy Harding got behind the wheel and gave me a reassuring glance in the rearview mirror. "It'll be all right, Emma."

I didn't answer, just turned to look at where Hatty and Rue stood on the porch of Glimmer Ridge, clinging to one another.

Look out for them. The man in my dreams claimed he could feel my anxiety, even when I wasn't in the house. Hopefully, he would keep Hatty and Rue out of this mess.

We drove through town just as the sun began to crest the eastern hills. Mist swirled down, thicker than usual. The heat from the vehicle did nothing to the chill that emanated from my marrow.

The ghost of Jody Haversham stood in front of the sheriff's office. It was a modular building that rested on cinderblocks. The deputy pulled around to the parking area that was surrounded by the chain-link fence. I stared at the ghost who didn't approach me, though he looked as though he had something to say.

"Come with me." I spoke the words out loud, hoping Jody would respond to the command and it would override my earlier order for him to stay away.

"If I can, I will." Art Harding mistakenly thought I was talking to him. "If not, I'll be right outside."

I nodded at him and forced a smile. The deputy was trying to go easy on me. It wasn't his fault that I'd bungled the situation, or that I'd given in to the ghost instead of doing what Hatty told me to do and mind my own damned business.

Deputy Harding escorted me into the building. To my relief, the ghost followed in our wake. I didn't know if he could help get me out of this soup, but it was better to have him close by in case a question cropped up that I couldn't successfully answer.

The sheriff's office was a converted three-bedroom ranch modular building. The common area held three desks, as well as the 911 call center. I recognized Sunshine Green, who stared at me with wide brown eyes as we moved past her into the main area. The second and third bedrooms had been converted into holding cells. The first was the sheriff's office. It was to that first bedroom that the deputy led me. He rapped lightly with two knuckles. The drawled, "Come in," carried through the door.

Sheriff Mac Yates was in his early fifties with assessing brown eyes and light brown hair shot through with silver. A thick mustache decorated his thin upper lip. He didn't smile the way he usually did when he popped by *Pages & Potions* for a coffee. Instead, he studied me as though he'd never seen me before. "Emma. Thank you for coming."

"It's not like I was given much choice." I wrapped my arms around myself.

The sheriff's expression turned rueful as he

explained, "I wanted to handle this as quickly and quietly as possible. There hasn't been a murder in this county in the last twenty years. Once word gets out, misinformation will spread. I need to get to the bottom of this before then. Have a seat." He gestured to the chair on the far side of his desk, which was neat as a pin. No hodgepodge of unsolved cases for Sheriff Yates in our little corner of the country.

I sat and wasn't surprised when he crossed the room and shut the door in Deputy Harding's face before coming over to perch against his desk, arms braced on either side of his lean hips. "Tell me about your relationship with Jody Haversham."

I had to fight the impulse to look at the ghost, who was bobbing up and down anxiously in the corner. "I didn't know him well."

"So why did you insist to Deputy Harding that something had happened to him?"

I shifted under his scrutiny. "He was missing. And everyone was acting like that was okay. If I went missing, I would hope that someone would at least look for me."

"Without a doubt, Hatty and Rue would call out the National Guard." He smiled tightly, but it faded when he said, "You've got a big heart, Emma. Now, I need to know everything you do about Jody Haversham and his work."

I told him about the podcast, claiming I'd stumbled across it by happenstance. I also mentioned going to see his sister because Jody had spoken of her to me.

The sheriff didn't need to know that had been after the man had died.

"I was in the area and thought maybe she'd heard from him. She said no, so I left."

"And that's all?" His knuckles turned white where they gripped the edge of the desk.

"That's all." At least all that he would believe.

A knock sounded on the outer door. "Sheriff, we've got a situation out here."

"I'll be right back," the sheriff gave me another tight smile and then stalked from the room, shutting the door behind him.

Not wanting to waste the chance, I rose and then circled the desk. I needed to know why the authorities were convinced that Jody Haversham was murdered. There were no convenient files for me to flip through, but a pixelated ball bounced around the desktop screen. I shook the mouse, waking the device up and hoping it wouldn't die the way Hatty's computer did anytime I touched it.

What I saw made my lips part. It was a photograph of a body on a metal table. The face looked so much different than the ghost, devoid of life. Jody's skin had grayed out, but that wasn't what caught my attention. The skin over his arms and chest and even one side of his face had been carved up into odd, swirling symbols. Beneath the image, the words *Cause of death: strangulation* and *carvings were done postmortem* snagged my gaze.

The screen flickered. I shivered and drew back.

Though I hated to ask him to look at his own corpse, I needed to know. "Jody, do you recognize these symbols?"

The ghost bobbed up behind me. "I can't...that is...I don't recall." He sounded uncertain.

Shit, he was beginning to fade. All apparitions did, though the timeline was as individual as the person. The first thing to go were the short-term memories, then long-term ones, and finally personalities until all that was left was a single raw emotion, like anger, sadness, or fear. Those were the kind that tended to haunt places that were familiar to them.

He seemed oddly detached as he stared at his own dead body. I turned to face him fully. "I'm so sorry this happened to you."

"Me too." His smile wobbled. "I'm glad you lifted the ban. I'm sorry I caused your accident. And that I didn't tell you about my wife."

"Where is she?" I breathed the question.

"I'm not sure." Jody shook his transparent head. "She has a place in Tennessee, but she travels a lot for her work. She's an artist."

"What's her name?"

"Tanya. Tanya Davis."

I blew out a breath and then pulled out my phone. Zooming in on the carved patterns and taking a series of photos, I captured the images before rounding to the far side of the desk. "Do you think she might have something to do with your death?"

The ghost drifted around the room as though he were lost in thought. "I'm not sure. We didn't part on the best of terms, but I'd hate to think she'd be involved with something like that." He nodded at the images on the computer screen.

I knew exactly what he meant. Before I decided if I ought to give Tanya's name to the sheriff, he re-entered the room. "Okay, Emma. You're free to go. I don't need to tell you that this conversation needs to stay between the two of us, do I?"

"No, sir." I rose and exited the office. Deputy Harding was nowhere in sight, but the 911 dispatcher, Sunshine Green, was just pulling on her blue coat. "Need a ride, Emma?"

I nodded, grateful. It would be a long time before I willingly climbed into a police vehicle again.

We didn't talk at all as she headed back into the more charming part of Mist Glen. I thanked Sunshine for the ride and then headed around the side alley. Jody Haversham floated nearby. I paused, meeting his gaze. "You've been found. I need to talk to Hatty and Rue. They're my best source of information on all things occult."

Jody nodded, though I could tell he wasn't pleased. "All right."

My key scraped across the lock when the kitchen door was yanked open from within. Hatty snagged my coat sleeve and then pulled me into her arms. I'd just begun to relax into her embrace when she gripped my shoulders and held me at a distance. She even shook me a little as she hissed, "What the hell is going on, Emma?"

I blew out a breath and accepted that I wasn't getting back to bed anytime soon.

"And you're sure that's everything?" Hatty asked. Her white hair was standing. Not surprising given that she'd been running her hands through it for the last hour as I gave the Bramblewick sisters a much more thorough report than I had shared with the sheriff. The only thing I kept to myself was that weird dream and the spirit of Glimmer Ridge calling me a mystic. No sense muddying the waters with things that may or may not be real.

"That's everything." I took a sip of the lemongrass and sage tea Rue had concocted, grateful for the soothing teaspoon of honey that eased my raw throat. Between the accident and the investigation, I'd spoken more in the past forty-eight hours than in the past four months. "I'm sorry I didn't tell you."

"It's all right, sweetness." Rue's hand covered mine. She was always the more maternal of the sisters, ready at a moment's notice to offer comfort to anyone in need.

"Don't coddle her." Hatty pushed away from the table and began to pace the tight confines of the kitchen. When she spoke again, she sounded breathless. "All this could have been avoided if you did as I told you and ignored the tagalongs."

"I know. I tried. But Jody was different. He already knew I could see him and—"

"And what?" Rue asked in a soft tone.

I swallowed and lifted my gaze to meet Hatty's piercing one. "No one else cared that he was gone. Nobody bothered to look for him. They were content for him to disappear as though he'd never existed. Just like me."

Utter silence filled the kitchen.

"Emma," Hatty began but didn't seem to know how to finish.

I shook my head. "It's been five years. And in all that time, not one person has come looking for me. No one asked about a woman who had given birth. Or the baby. Not a single clue to my past has surfaced. No one cares. Or if they did, they were content to believe I'd died." The last word came out as a sob.

"Oh, sweetness." Rue rose and crushed me to her pillowy softness. "It's all right."

It wasn't, though. I'd been thrown away. No wonder I'd gone to the ridiculous lengths I had for Jody. We were two of a kind. Disposable. My shoulders shook as emotion swept through me, an intense storm long overdue.

Gradually, the sobs died down, leaving me exhausted.

"Why didn't you tell us you felt this way?" Hatty croaked as though her throat was clogged.

I wiped my eyes on my pajama sleeve. "Because you two have sacrificed so much to take me in. I didn't want you to think I was ungrateful for everything you've done."

"We could never think that." Rue petted my hair.

I sniffled and looked up at the Bramblewicks. "I know it isn't right to ask you two to put yourselves out any further, but do you think you could help me?"

"With what?" Hatty's brows drew down. "Jody's been found. As horrific as it is, that was what he wanted."

"Yes, but he's still here."

"Like here *here*?" Rue yelped and swung her head from side to side.

I nodded.

"Where?" Hatty squinted as though that would allow her to see the ghost.

I gestured to the corner where Jody Haversham had been listening while I explained everything.

They turned in unison, two sets of blue eyes searching.

"Yes." Hatty exhaled wearily. "We're sorry, Jody. We'll do whatever we can to catch your killer."

I jolted at that. Killer. Man, I was slow. Somehow, I hadn't put together the fact that Jody Haversham had been murdered with the notion that someone had killed him. Someone had strangled him to death and then carved those horrific symbols into his flesh.

And I'd just dragged the Bramblewicks into unmasking the villain.

"Maybe we shouldn't—" I began, but Hatty cut me off.

"Rue, I want you to research death symbols. The fact that they were carved after he died must mean something. Emma, you and I are going to investigate Jody's digital files. He'll give us all his passwords so we can access email and the like."

"What are we looking for?" I frowned.

"Threats," Hatty's tone turned grim. "You were on the right track before. Dollars to doughnuts someone other than Jody's sister didn't like his blog content. And if that person reached out, we might have a lead to hand over to the sheriff."

"What about the wife?" I asked.

"She'll be the first person the police investigate," Hatty said. "But my gut is telling me that even if she had the motive, this has something to do with the podcast. Witches have always been scapegoats. Along with anyone who advocated for their well-being and fair treatment. And our ghostly friend falls into that category."

Rue looked between us. "So, when should we start?"

"*Carpe diem*," Hatty said.

"What about the store?" Rue asked over a yawn. "I'm supposed to be making sour cream and chive scones right now, not digging through the archives searching for death runes."

Hatty threw her hands in the air. "Oh fine. I'll show Emma. We'll multitask."

"Show Emma what?" I glanced between the two of them.

Hatty rose and gestured for me to follow. She put on her parka, pulling the faux fur-lined hood over her unruly white hair. My coat was still on, though it was unzipped. Side by side, we headed out the back door. Instead of turning toward the street as I expected, Hatty strode purposefully toward the old potting shed at the far corner of the property.

"Um, Hatty?" I asked as she fumbled with the combination lock. We were both still sporting our pajamas. Screwing around in the yard was bound to raise a few eyebrows.

"Ah ha!" Hatty exclaimed, and a moment later, the lock sprung free. "The combo is two ten one. The year we inherited Glimmer Ridge. Remember that."

"Mkay," I said slowly. "But why do I need to know it now when I haven't needed it in the last five years?"

"You weren't ready." Hatty stood back and gestured for me to go ahead of her.

"Ready? For what?" My words broke off as I stared around the dim interior.

The "shed" was a front for a doorway that led to stone steps that looked like nothing more than mushrooms growing from a massive tree. Hatty snapped her fingers and torches flared to life.

"What is this?" I stared at her as if I'd never seen her before.

"Magic," she grinned. "Welcome to the Lair. Come on. You have a lot to learn."

CHAPTER
SEVEN

The torches emitted light, but no heat. I shoved my icy hands deep into my coat pockets as we made our way down the spongy fungal stairs into the heart of the Lair. They even felt springy under my sneakers.

"How long has this been here?" I asked Hatty as we trekked downward.

"As long as Glimmer Ridge has. From my research, it looks like our predecessors dug out the cellar at the same time as they put this in."

Unlike the house, there were no flourishes of architecture. This space was minimalistic. Designed for function. There was no mortar between the stones. They were stacked perfectly. The closest I'd come to seeing anything like it was in old issues of National Geographic.

Finally, the mushroom stairs ended. Hatty stepped aside, allowing me to take a look around the space. It was a large room, roughly the size of a two-car garage. One wall was lined entirely with floor-to-ceiling bookshelves with live edges. Another held spell jars of every shape and size. A hanging rack that looked like some sort of medieval torture device held dried bunches of sage, lavender, and rosemary, as well as a few other herbs I couldn't identify. Three different workstations had been set up around the room. One was a fire pit on the southern wall, the one farthest away from the books. Another held what looked like half of an oversized clamshell. The third side sported a collection of crystals and geodes. A large pentagram surrounded by a circle was carved into the exact center of the floor and coated in what looked like brick dust.

I turned in a circle, trying to take it all in. "This is incredible."

Hatty smiled proudly. "We would have brought you here sooner, but you had so much to deal with already, so many changes. It was better for you to think we were nutty dabblers instead of actual witches."

Our gazes locked. "And you can do magic?"

Her chin tilted up with pride. "Nothing flashy. Rue and I aren't all that powerful. We mostly work with energy and intention. But you, Emma…"

The way she was staring made me swallow. "What about me?"

"You can see ghosts. Communicate with them. We both sensed your ability the first night you came to Glimmer Ridge. You have a gift."

A gift? "Seeing ghosts isn't magic, though. People see them all the time."

She shook her head slowly. "Not as frequently as you. There's more to it. I've been researching but I haven't figured out what you are yet. Magic swirls around you all the time. It's part of the reason I've been urging you to lie low. Anyone with the sight could pick up on your aura a mile away."

"The sight?"

"Second sight. It's a way to find ley lines and to sense auras. I'll teach you how later. For now, we need to do what we came here to do. These are the archives." Hatty moved to the wall of books. Her arthritic fingers caressed several different spines before she finally pulled one free and carried it back to where I stood.

"Death runes in the modern age." I read the title.

"It's a way for magical practitioners—witches—to give themselves a power boost. Carving runes into a victim."

I gaped at her as horror filled me. "Have you ever done that?"

"No." Hatty shook her head vehemently. "Neither Rue nor I are interested in expanding our gifts, especially not if it harms another person. Our creed has always been, *And harm to none, do what thou wilt.*"

Relieved, I opened the book to a random page. The death runes were odd, with sharp angles like capital letters or triangles. I extracted my phone from my back pocket and compared the photos I'd taken to the drawings on the page. "The ones on Jody's body are more...swirly."

Hatty glanced over my shoulder. "Swirly. Hmm. I guess that makes sense. These sorts of death runes are intended for use on a living victim." Hatty took the book out of my numb hands before I dropped it.

"Careful, Emma," she chided. "Most of the items in this space are replaceable. The books, though, are one of a kind." She set it carefully back on the shelf. "I have a few others I want to look into, but we need to get back and open the store. If you're up for it?"

"Yeah." Taking one last glance around, I studied the stack of jars full of moon water. "I always wondered what you did with all that water you set out for the full moon."

"That's Rue's doing. It can be used in pretty much any kind of spell and makes kick-ass cocktails." Hatty ushered me forward and together we climbed up out of the magic archives via the fungi stairs and onto the ground floor.

Hatty's breathing sounded particularly laborious. She paused at one point as a coughing fit overtook her.

I hovered over her. "Is there anything I can do?"

She waved away my concern. "It's fine, Emma. The winter air is sharp. I'm not thirty anymore. Aging, one star, would not recommend."

My lips twitched. "Hey, it beats the alternative, right?" I offered her an arm as we emerged from the potting shed/witchy hideout and back to the house.

"I'll take care of the store," I told her as we entered

the warm confines of the kitchen. Rue paused in the middle of kneading dough. Her apron was covered with smears of flour and she had a smudge across her creased forehead. "Did you find anything?"

I pulled out a chair for Hatty, and she collapsed into it with obvious relief. "Not the sort of death runes we have in the archives. Emma, is Jody still here?"

I glanced around the kitchen. "I don't see him. But sometimes the tagalongs fade if they're lost in thought. Want me to open the shop?"

"If you would. I think I'll use a little of my illicit witchery and take a hot bath."

That had my eyebrows climbing to my hairline. "With our temperamental water heater?"

"That's what makes it illicit," Rue explained with a wink.

"As in evil?" I'd had so much thrown at me that I didn't know where to begin or what questions to ask.

"No, honey. Hatty and I are what are known in the circles as gray witches. We perform self-serving magic. Things to make our lives a little easier." Rue wiped her cheek, leaving another streak of flour behind.

"*And harm to none, do what thou wilt,*" I repeated the phrase Hatty had told me down in the Lair. I nodded in understanding, then scowled. "Wait a second. You're telling me I've been taking lukewarm showers for the last five years for no good reason?"

Hatty chuckled. "No, dearest. The shower is what it is until we manage to scrape together enough money to replace the water heater. A bathtub, though, is like nothing more than a really big cauldron. I'll show you the heating charm later. Just don't use it when you're already in the tub or you'll cook your own goose."

Second sight and a heating charm. A witchy lair I'd known nothing about. My mind whirled. "Okay, I need to run upstairs and change before we open. Do either of you need anything?"

They shook their heads.

I pushed out of the kitchen and then headed for the stairs. My entire body ached, but it was of secondary concern to my overloaded mind.

The Bramblewicks were witches. Who could do magic. All this time I'd thought of them as quirky women who liked to stand out. But the Lair...it was like nothing I'd ever seen before. Well, at least that I remembered.

Slowly, I walked into my room and shut the door. With my hand on the rough-hewn wall, I called out, "And you? What are you hiding from me?"

No answer.

"Glimmer Ridge, sexy guy," I said. Nothing.

Frustrated, I slapped the wall, ignoring the sting in my palm. "Hey, dude. I'm talking to you."

Still no answer.

"Be that way," I mumbled and then stripped off my pajamas.

Real? Figment? How could I tell the difference?

SINCE IT WAS Saturday and the weather had turned to a gray drizzle, *Pages & Potions* was full to bursting. We had a local author in to read and answer questions about his new release. I listened as I made coffee, enjoying snippets from his book of local legends and fables. Appalachia was full of all sorts of ghost stories. It reminded me of Jody's podcast.

I froze in the middle of what I was doing. The podcast, of course. I'd have to find out if Jody mentioned anything about runes in the podcast. My to-do list was growing by the day. It was frightening but also exciting. I felt like a butterfly that had been trapped inside a chrysalis and was getting the first real peek at the outside world.

"I think that's good, Emma." Sissy nodded toward the counter.

Coffee overflowed the mug and ran down the counter. "Oh shoot. Sorry."

She lifted her plate that held the crumbs from one of Rue's scones. "Is everything okay? You seem distracted."

"Fine," I smiled. "You're spending a lot of time in here lately."

"Honestly, it's the most welcoming place in town. Most of the locals ignore me when I go into the diner or anywhere else. I thought the South was supposed to be hospitable."

"It is," I told her and then paused. "Actually, it might take people a while to warm up and accept you. So yeah, you're welcome to hang out here as long as you like."

She flashed me a relieved grin that showed off her dimples. "So tell me, how did your date go?"

I checked the area around us but all the patrons were either listening to the guest author or browsing the shelves. "Fine. We aren't a love match."

"So you wouldn't mind if I went out with him?" She raised a brow.

I blinked. "Really?"

"I won't ask him if you're against it. Bra code and all." She winked. "There is a serious shortage of datable dudes in this place. And I already made the mistake of dating a single dad of one of my students. Never again."

"It's fine with me." I shrugged. "I'll even throw you a bridal shower. Rue can make her infamous penis pops."

We giggled until Hatty cast us a dirty look from over by the mystery section.

"Sorry," I mouthed at her.

"I better go before I get you in trouble." Sissy picked up her hobo bag and then waved. "Maybe we can hang out some night? Do a girl's movie night or something?"

"Sounds good. Though we don't have streaming here. Rue and Hatty refuse to cut the cord."

"No problem, I picked up a monkey butt ton of DVDs at a garage sale so we've got options." She winked. "This is gonna be fun."

My heart leapt. A girl's night in with someone close to my age. It was something that I'd always wanted. "Just let me know what night you're free."

"Will do." With a final wave, Sissy donned her parka and then headed out the door.

The next few hours flew by. I filled out order forms for books we didn't carry and needed to special order. Frothed milk for hot beverages. Cleaned up crumbs and reorganized books in the used section that Mist Glen residents could swap out for store credit. I rang up sales and sanded the walkway, so no one slipped on their way in or out. The temperature was dropping, and refreeze was imminent. That meant black ice and sore asses.

Emma.

I paused in the middle of pouring hot water over a chamomile and peppermint blend. A fast glance around told me there was no one nearby. Everyone in my line of sight appeared fine and dandy. But I felt sure I'd heard a man's pain-filled voice.

My sense of disquiet grew as the day wore on. Something was off, but for the life of me, I couldn't figure out what or where. I checked on Hatty and Rue so often that Hatty finally ordered me to take out the trash and stop bugging her.

Finally, it was time to flip the sign from open to closed. The second I touched the door, it washed through me. Agony. Wave after wave of it crested over me until my knees almost buckled.

Mother moon. Staggering back from the door, realization dawned. The voice, the sensation of gnawing pain. That was him—Glimmer Ridge. With one hand still wrapped around my midsection, I headed for the stairs.

"Emma?" Hatty called as the smell of stew wafted out of the kitchen.

I was already halfway up. "Go ahead and eat without me. I'm going to lie down for a spell."

Not waiting for a reply, I stumbled to my room and shut the door. When I leaned against it, I spoke out loud to the house. "What's the matter?"

The second I made direct contact, pain ripped through my system like barbed wire through my veins. I collapsed onto the floor in a heap.

Some untold amount of time later, I awoke on the beach. This time, though, the mist had thinned. The dull roar of the ocean and the cry of gulls combined with the tang of salty sea air filled my senses. I could feel the spirit of Glimmer Ridge but didn't see any sign of him.

"Where are you?" I called out.

A groan sounded. It seemed to be coming from all around me.

"Talk to me." I turned in a circle and picked a direction at random.

If he'd been a snake, I would have stepped on him. As it was, I tripped over what felt like his legs. On my hands and knees, I crawled closer. Though I still couldn't see him, I felt my way up from the leg to his bare hip, then up his torso, and finally to what I assumed was his face.

"What's wrong with you?"

An image of light green irises the color of sea glass filled my mind as he rasped, "Dying."

"What?" That couldn't be possible. "Why? What can I do to help you?" The male, whatever he was, had been my comfort and protector for the last five years. I didn't want to think about what I would do without him.

A hand traveled up my arm, pausing at my shoulder. "Starving. Too long since I last fed."

He was starving to death? "Why didn't you say something before? I could have brought you something to eat." Though I wasn't a hundred percent sure about that. I wasn't even sure I had physically entered the dreamscape, never mind if I could carry something solid like a peanut butter and jelly sandwich with me.

The image of that eerie green gaze flickered through my mind as invisible fingers speared into my hair. It felt as light as the sea breeze that lifted locks of hair from my face. "I'm glad I could see you again one last time."

I curled my fingers over his. A tear slipped down my face. "Tell me how to help you. There's got to be something I can do?"

"I won't. Against my vows," he rasped.

"You took vows not to eat?" His words didn't make sense. He'd called out. I was the only one who could hear him. There had to be some way for me to help him.

Another breeze-like caress stroked the curve of my cheekbone. "I don't want to feed from you, Emma. Enough has been taken from you."

Feed from me? My mind whirled. "Are you a vampire of some kind? Do you need blood?"

"Not blood. Energy," he groaned.

"Energy," I repeated. "How do I give it to you? Please, tell me."

His next words chilled me to the bone. "With an orgasm."

EIGHT

I rocked back out of reach of him as my heart rate quadrupled. "Is that some sort of line?"

He shifted beneath my hands as if he were trying to move away. "Knew you wouldn't...believe me."

"Stay still," I snapped, beyond frustrated. "What are you? Tell me once and for all."

"Incubus." The word rattled out of him like the clatter of old bones.

An incubus. I'd read about them, though I hadn't thought they were real. An incubus was a male demon that fed on sexual release. No wonder my dreams of him had been so sensual.

I braced myself for the answer. "And when was the last time you...fed?"

"Over five years ago," he whispered.

My lips parted. "Why? Are you trapped here?"

"In a way," he hedged.

So I was his only source of nutrition?

Yes, something inside me whispered. *That's as it should be.*

Whatever that voice was, it had no sense of self-preservation. But could I just sit here and watch him die?

Calm washed over me like the waves lap against the shore. "Then you need to feed off me."

"No," he coughed, choked. "No Emma. I won't use you like that."

"It's not using me if I offer." Would I have to convince him of this? Keeping one hand on his invisible form, I began dragging my sweater up over my head. "It's okay..." Mother Moon, I didn't even know his name.

As though reading my thoughts, he breathed, "Z."

"Z," I repeated.

Those sea-green eyes that I could only see in my mind slid shut, as though hearing me speak his name gave him pleasure.

But it was my pleasure he needed. My orgasm. And I hadn't had one in the last five years. The only times I'd even been close were when I thought of him. Damn it, I was not the right woman for the job.

But there was no one else.

"Stay right where you are," I commanded him. Not bothering to wait for a reply, I stripped the sweater up over my head and then tackled the snap on my jeans. When I was down to just my underwear, I reached for him again, feeling along the invisible length of his arms until I located his hands. And then I guided them to me.

His palms closed over my breasts. I arched into the perfection of his touch, loving the feel of being cupped that way. He caressed me gently, his breaths still full of that ugly rattle.

"More," I panted and reached behind my back to unhook the bra. The straps loosened, and I shrugged until they slid down over my shoulders.

"Emma," he whispered. I moved his hands out of the way and took the bra off before replacing his palms. A hiss of pleasure escaped me as he touched my naked skin.

My eyes slid shut as his thumbnails scraped lightly over my puckered nipples, sending a jolt of need arrowing straight between my legs.

"More." Without conscious thought, I threw a leg over him until I was straddling my invisible lover. Who was this bold hussy who knew exactly what she wanted, what he needed? Awash in sensation, I took it all in. Taut stomach muscles flexed under me. His breaths grew louder, and his hands traveled to my hips, guiding me into place above a massive erection.

I remember this. Not actively, but the way muscles recalled learning to balance on a bike. The sensation of being touched, of yearning for release, of needing just a little bit more.

He split me perfectly with his invisible shaft. The head bumped along my clit, making me moan. I wanted nothing more than to look down, to see him.

But there was nothing to see. I could feel the hot, hard length as it pressed along the seam of my body. Only my underwear separated my slick heat from taking him deep inside me.

"Ride me, petal," his tone was commanding. His hands traced up along my sides and then slid back to my ass, guiding me against him. I rocked forward and back. The motion made his shaft stroke me perfectly. "That's it, love."

My core clenched and found only emptiness. "I'm close."

"Emma," he rasped. A flash of that light green gaze filled my vision. My eyes slid shut a moment before my release barreled over me with the impact of a freight train. My back arched, and I cried out as it surged on and on and *on*.

I hovered there on the precipice as gold mist erupted from my body. Suspended in the throes, I whispered, "What?"

"It's the energy you released," he murmured.

"That's what you feed from?" It was beautiful, but it seemed to be fading. "Take it."

"Emma—" his tone sounded pleading.

What was he waiting for? "Take it," I snapped. "Otherwise, I did this for nothing."

A moment's hesitation where I was sure he would refuse. Then the sound of a long, slow draw. The air pressure around us seemed to shift and the glittering mist was drawn down into the being I straddled. It hovered for a moment and then vanished.

Relieved, I rolled to the side and shut my eyes. Sand pressed into my bare skin and despite the warm sunshine, I shivered.

A hand caressed my shoulder. "Are you all right?"

Was I? I didn't know. Nothing was the way I'd believed when I went to bed the night before. Jody Haversham had been murdered. Hatty and Rue were witches. And my tireless companion, Glimmer Ridge, was an incubus who'd just fed from me.

With my lids still lowered, I whispered, "Do you feel better?"

A fingertip trailed over my bottom lip. "Much. You can see me now."

I hesitated. Why was I suddenly afraid? After the way I'd exposed myself to him, it seemed foolish. But still, anxiety rolled through me in waves. What if he didn't live up to my fantasies? There was a shroud of safety in thinking that the man in my dreams, the voice of Glimmer Ridge, was only a figment of my imagination.

That safety had been violently ripped away.

Z didn't speak. He waited patiently for me to nut up. With a sigh of acceptance, I raised my lids and studied my fantasy lover.

The thought rose unbidden, *He's even more magnificent than in my imagination.* Thick, dark hair cascaded around his brawny shoulders. His lips were lush and kissable, more than I'd ever seen on a man. His jaw was strong but smooth, with no trace of stubble.

My gaze traveled down over tightly packed muscle. His body was hairless everywhere save for on top of his head. His skin was perfectly unmarred, an entrancing golden color that made me feel like I dwelled in a cave. Above his hip, right beside the jutting erection I'd ridden to ecstasy, there sat a circular mark. Not a tattoo. A brand. Horror filled me. The puckered flesh was raised, forming the scar. The small circle was filled with writing that I didn't recognize.

He shifted as though my looking at the mark made him uncomfortable. My gaze snagged on his still hard shaft. Oh man, he didn't come. I felt like a bitch, using him the way I did, as though he was some sort of sex toy.

An apology on my lips, my gaze flew to his. A jolt went through me.

Those eyes. Exactly how I'd been picturing them. His irises were the lightest green, the color of sea glass with tiny golden flecks. Captivating. And they filled with a sorrow that burrowed under my skin and took root next to mine.

My teeth sank into my lower lip. "You know me from before I came here." It was not a question, so I didn't phrase it like one.

The voice I knew so well, the one that filled my dreams, answered, "Yes."

A lump formed in my throat. "How long before?'

"We met that night." His breath rose and fell as those eerie irises scanned my face. As though he could read my mind, he murmured, "I'm not the father of your babe, Emma."

My gaze fell from his as I whispered, "Do you know what happened to my child?"

"No." That deep voice rumbled through my skin until it made my marrow quake. "The babe was gone by the time I arrived."

I rolled onto my back and then covered my face with my hands. A sob broke free, followed by another. It was as though the orgasm I'd experienced pulverized the cork that had been stoppering up all my grief, my pain, and my fear.

Z pulled me into his arms and held me close. Unlike when I touched the walls of Glimmer Ridge, he didn't speak or try to soothe me. He held me and let me cry it out.

As though he understood that was exactly what I needed.

Finally, I sniffled and drew back. "How did you know what I am? A mystic you said."

He tucked a strand of hair behind my ear. "I'm afraid that's my fault."

"How so?"

He took a deep breath and then rolled onto his back. "To save you, I had to share my essence with you. It's why you can hear me, even when you can't see me."

I blinked. "You mean you made it so I could see the ghosts?"

"No." He sat up and then reached for my hand. "A

mystic is someone who has stared death in the face, then returned. My essence brought you back, Emma, but the fact that you died is what gives you your abilities."

A lump formed in my throat. "Why did you save me?"

For the first time, he looked away, turning toward the endless expanse of sea. "My reasons are my own."

I licked my lips. "Is saving me the reason I haven't been able to see you?"

A muscle ticked in that firm jaw. I was getting the impression that he wasn't going to answer any other questions.

For now, anyway.

Leaning forward, I brushed a kiss across his cheek. "Thank you for saving my life."

His head turned, and I saw the surprise on his features a moment before the beach faded from view.

I STAYED in bed the next morning, sorting through all I had learned. The voice that had been comforting me for the last five years was real. I'd thought he was the spirit of the house, something generations of Bramblewicks had imparted into the structure. But no, Z was a being imprisoned within the walls of Glimmer Ridge. An incubus. And whatever he had done to save my life had trapped him there, I was sure of it.

I wasn't sure what to think about...feeding him. I hadn't believed I could be so bold. But instinct had taken over. There had been no shame, no self-recrimination. In a way, it was fitting that the first orgasm I could remember was with him. Thankfully, I'd had enough sense to keep my underwear on, otherwise I would have taken him inside me. I knew I wasn't ready to make love.

Hell, I'd just learned his name. But feeding him... well, didn't I owe him since he was so depleted because he'd helped me? Besides, it wasn't exactly a hardship to be with him sexually. He was the only being I'd felt that sort of carnal attraction for since I'd arrived at *Pages & Potions*.

A knock sounded on my door. "Emma? Are you all right?"

"Yeah, Rue. I'll be down in a few." Tossing the covers aside, I rose to dress. When my hand accidentally brushed the doorframe, Glimmer Ridge—Z— purred, *Good morning, petal*.

"Good morning." I gave the doorframe a caress. "How often do you...?" I trailed off, not sure how to phrase what I wanted to know.

How often must I feed you? In my mind's eye, I could see one of those dark eyebrows rise. *Don't trouble yourself with that, Emma. I am here for you whenever you need me.*

"That's not an answer." Annoyed, I removed my

hand from the doorframe and focused on pulling a long-sleeved t-shirt over my head. "I'll come back to you later and we'll talk more."

I'll await your return.

The store was closed for the day. The Bramblewick sisters and I gathered in the kitchen.

"Breakfast is in the microwave," Rue told me as she sipped her tea, which smelled of lavender and bergamot.

I opened the microwave door and smiled at the plate, which smiled back. "I can't remember the last time you made chocolate chip pancakes."

Rue shrugged. "I figured after the week you've had, you could use the boost."

"You figured right." Sitting down at the table, I ignored the bottle of pure maple syrup and instead reached for the can of whipped cream. Dessert for breakfast—just what the doctor ordered.

"So, what's our battle plan?" I asked Hatty, who had a yellow legal pad in front of her.

She studied me for a long moment. "According to what you found out, we have three avenues to research. The runes on Jody Haversham's body, his podcast messages, and his wife."

"Are we ruling out the sister?" Rue asked and reached to spoon some sourwood honey into her tea.

"I'm not sure." I glanced around, but there was no sign of Jody's ghost. "She was agitated by my coming by and asking questions. And she didn't seem concerned about him, the way you two would be if someone told you your sibling was missing for days."

Rue frowned. "So, which should we investigate first?" She appeared almost giddy at the thought of mixing in with a murder investigation.

"I say we divide and conquer." Hatty drummed her sharp nails on the Formica table. "The runes in the archives were a bust so Rue, you can contact the coven and ask about other images. I'll see what I can do to crack Jody Haversham's cloud account. Emma, it's up to you, the sister or the wife?"

"His sister already knows my face. I doubt I'll learn anything more from her." Scraping the last smear of chocolate and whipped cream off my plate, I popped the fork in my mouth and then rose. "I'll check into the wife."

Then I frowned. "Wait, we don't have a car anymore. How will I get to Tennessee?"

The sisters exchanged a glance. "What would you think about asking Sissy?"

I blew out a sigh, but Hatty rose. "Before you say no, Emma, I want you to know we've done a reading on Sissy. Your fates are entwined."

I scowled at her. "What do you mean, a reading?"

"With a lock of her hair," Rue chirped.

"Does she know you did this?" I gaped at the Bramblewicks.

Hatty waved me off. "Oh pish. People do background checks all the time, so what's the difference?"

Where to begin? I shook my head. "The difference

is you used a piece of her body, not some random info she typed up on social media. Besides, I don't want to involve Sissy if I don't have to. We're talking about hunting down a killer. She's a Kindergarten teacher."

"Fine then, what's your suggestion for our transportation issue?" Hatty lifted her brows and waited.

A light bulb inside my brain switched on. "I have an idea."

Hatty and Rue exchanged a glance. "More frightening words have never been spoken."

CHAPTER
NINE

"Thank you so much," I said to Mrs. Otis as she handed me the keys to ol' Bessie, her VW bus. Jody's car—the ride I'd intended to borrow—had been impounded by the sheriff's office. But when I explained what I wanted, the widow offered me an alternative.

"Oh, you're doing me the favor." Mrs. Otis looked like a child wrapped in her ankle-length red coat. "I don't run her nearly as often as I should. You know how to drive a stick shift?"

I did. It was one of those muscle memory skills that had stayed with me even as all my details remained hidden.

Like riding Z.

Shut up, brain, I snapped mentally and then forced out, "Yup."

The heater on the bus was for shit, but I was garbed to stave off even a mountain winter in a heavy coat, hat, gloves, and a scarf that covered my mouth and nose. After backing the bus out of the barn, I did a broken K turn and rolled down the gravel drive toward the village.

Instead of turning toward *Pages & Potions*, I steered out onto the main road that led away from Mist Glen and headed west. The ghost appeared as I paused at a stop light.

"Emma," Jody Haversham began. "I think you're barking up the wrong tree here."

"Maybe," I acknowledged as the bus putt-putted along. "But since you aren't giving me anything else to go on, I might as well find her and ask a few questions. Anything you can give me to help?"

"We've been separated for about five years," the ghost admitted, as though it pained him.

"Five years?" It was probably a coincidence that Jody and his wife had called it quits around the same time I came to Mist Glen. "Was there a reason?"

The apparition shrugged. "We grew apart, is all. It happens."

I drew my own conclusions by the way he clammed up. He was still trying to protect the woman, even from the far side of the grave. Jody still loved her.

My thoughts returned to Z. Men were strange and unfathomable creatures. I wondered if other women thought so. I'd have to ask Sissy during our girl's night, leaving out the ghost and incubus bits, of course.

The ride took longer than it would have in Hatty's truck, but that was fine with me. A little thrill shot through me as I turned onto roads I hadn't ever been on before, at least not in memory.

The ice from the other day was a distant memory, and the sun shone down on me as the bus rolled downhill. I passed trucks and commuter vehicles as I crossed the state line. Jody instructed me once I reached the town of Gobbler's Ridge. It was a larger version of Mist Glen, one that had chain restaurants and even a motel. I spotted a Starbucks sign as well as several fast food and gas stations.

After filling up Ol' Bessie—who had burned through almost half a tank in under an hour—I turned off the county road to a dirt and gravel one that was badly in need of repair. My molars clanked together as I hit yet another pothole. Hopefully, I wouldn't crack an axle. It would be embarrassing to phone the Bramblewicks and tell them I'd been stranded.

"Turn here," the ghost of Jody Haversham indicated the left fork in the road that grew even smaller and was filled with dozens of potholes. I made the turn and then crested a rise. The summit overlooked the bowl of a valley and an L-shaped ranch house.

Smoke billowed from the chimney. I frowned as I drew closer. That was a lot of smoke.

"Tanya!" Jody shouted and then vanished.

It took me way too long to realize what was happening. Then my brain shrieked, *Mother Moon, the house is on fire!*

I parked the bus as close as I dared to come to the

house and fumbled for my cell. No signal. Of fucking course.

Climbing from the van, I spun in a circle, hoping to get a bar so I could call 911. Nothing.

Jody appeared on the porch. "She's unconscious in the kitchen. Please, Emma, help her."

Hatty would have my guts for garters if I stormed into a burning building. But what choice did I have? I couldn't let her die. Taking a deep breath, I tucked the ends of my scarf into my coat and made sure they covered my nose and mouth before following the dead man in to save his wife.

The door handle was cool to the touch. I twisted it and relief filled me to find it unlocked. Choking black smoke billowed out, obscuring Jody's transparent form.

I took one final breath of fresh mountain air before following him into the house.

Fires are loud. Judging from the direction smoke billowed from the left side and the creak of timbers, that was where the blaze had begun, and where it raged the hottest. Squinting in the gloom, I spotted a flicker I thought was Jody and followed it, almost tripping on the body that lay before the door.

"Ms. Davis!" I shouted and shook her shoulder.

Her lips were parted, dry, and cracked. Her head lolled, but I spied the pulse throbbing in her throat. The scent of gin wafted from her mouth.

Fan-frigging-tastic. I coughed and then gripped her under the arms. At the same time, a great crashing noise sounded from behind me. My heart pounded so hard and I grew lightheaded. Was that the roof caving in?

On instinct, I turned, dragging Tanya Davis's body away from the propped-open kitchen door, slamming it shut and cutting off the onslaught of smoke. There was no other door to the room, but a foggy window sat above the kitchen table. I ran to it but it didn't open. It was a single pane of glass meant to let light in, not air.

I stared out, trying to come up with a plan. I couldn't drag her out to the front, but the house was built so it backed into a rolling hill. We were only a few feet above the ground. Glancing around, I spied a cast-iron skillet on the stovetop. I picked it up and tested its weight. That ought to work.

Aiming for the center, I flung the skillet with all my strength.

A loud crash heralded the window's demise. It was an older pane of glass, not safety glass. It shattered, leaving jagged edges like teeth hanging down or poking up. I lay on my back and kicked the loose shards and the aluminum frame clear of the new opening before hauling Tanya Davis's inert form onto the table.

The smoke grew thicker in the kitchen. I was sweating like a hog in a sauna by the time I levered her up to the window. I shoved her slipper-clad feet out first. She was built like me, though—bottom-heavy. It took an extra push to scoot her bottom over the sill. I lost my grip, and she slid to the ground in a heap.

I aimed my own feet to the left of her, hoping I wouldn't fall directly on top of the unconscious woman. Then, pushing off, gravity snagged me and dragged my carcass down. My teeth clacked together and my sore ribs sang painfully as I landed on the frozen ground.

After dragging in several lungfuls of fresh air, I rolled back to face Tanya Davis. She was covered with grass and bits of glass, but as I turned her over, she let out a soft snore.

"You've got...awful taste...in women..." I huffed to the ghost who bobbed along anxiously as I dragged Tanya farther away from the burning house. What remained of the roof was engulfed in flames and as I paused to catch my breath, it caved in.

"Thank you." Jody Haversham kneeled beside his wife as though trying to caress her blotchy, soot-stained face.

"Don't mention it," I rasped and sagged against the van.

An hour later, I sat in the visitor's waiting area while Tanya Davis was treated for smoke inhalation. Miraculously, neither of us had been seriously injured. The white-haired doctor gave me an odd look when he spotted the fading yellow and green bruises on my face. "Are you sure you're all right?"

"Rough week. I've had worse though." I rasped and then gestured to the curtained-off area where Tanya lay. "How is she?"

"Drunk as a skunk." The doctor shook his head. "Probably lit a candle or left a towel on the radiator and then passed out. She's lucky to be alive. Thanks to you."

"When can I talk to her?" After all that we'd gone through, I wasn't about to turn tail and head back to Mist Glen without asking her about Jody.

"Probably an hour or so. We're pushing fluids." He patted me on the knee and then bustled off.

My ribs screamed as I got up and headed over to the soda machine. My esophagus felt as though I'd deep-throated a spruce branch, so the last thing I wanted was something carbonated. Or hot. Bottled water, it would be.

Swallowing was a painful exercise, but the water tasted delicious. When I returned to check on her, the ghost hovered around Tanya's bed. Maybe it was a coincidence that Jody's estranged wife had been in a fire the week after his death. But somehow, I doubted it.

"Who knows about her?" I asked the apparition.

"Just my sister, you, and the Bramblewicks. I never talked about her on the podcast."

"Any reason someone would come after her?" I asked.

The ghost shook his head. "No. I started the podcast after we separated. As far as I know, she didn't even know about it."

Damn it, was it a coincidence? A house fire was a far cry from carving odd symbols into a body.

Unless...an unnerving thought occurred. What if Tanya had killed Jody? Perhaps she'd been drinking to forget, and the fire had been an accident.

Sagging into the uncomfortable generic furniture, I tried to breathe shallowly. I wouldn't get any answers until she woke up and started talking.

I must have dozed off because the next thing I knew, I was blinking over at the opened curtain and an empty hospital bed. I rose and turned in a circle, my sneakers squeaking on the floor. "Hello?"

A young woman in green scrubs jogged up. "What's wrong?"

I pointed at the empty bed. "Where is Tanya Davis?" Maybe she'd been taken somewhere for tests.

The nurse made a face. "She checked out about half an hour ago against medical advice."

My heart sank. "Any idea where she went?"

"Sorry." She did a palms-up and turned to go.

Damn it all to hell and back. I sagged back onto the uncomfortable couch.

Why did Tanya leave? And where had she gone? My phone chimed, letting me know I had an incoming text.

Hatty: I got through your tagalong's firewall. He had more than a dozen threats lodged in his email. Rue turned up a few more runes for you to look at. Will you be home for dinner?

I made a face and then typed back, *Almost done here. Be back soon.*

An hour later I was coaxing ol' Bessie into Mrs. Otis's barn just as Deputy Harding pulled up behind me.

"Emma!" he called, waving me over toward his car.

I blew out a breath and then dredged up a smile I didn't feel. "Hey, Art. How's it going?"

"Good, good." He put the car in park, clambered out, and caught up with me. "Listen, I'm real sorry about the other night. I hope the sheriff didn't grill you too badly."

I waved it off and began to walk toward the humpbacked bridge, hoping he'd get the hint. "You're just doing your job, right?"

Dismay filled me at the sound of a car door being slammed. Then he was striding alongside me over the bridge. "I'm really not supposed to talk about it, but seeing as we've got the suspect in custody, I guess I can tell you. We just found out that Jody Haversham had a million-dollar life insurance policy."

That snagged my attention. "Wow. Who was named as the beneficiary?"

"His wife."

My lips parted. Luckily, Art Harding mistook the

source of my shock. "I know, right? No one here knew he was even married!"

"That's something," I breathed. "So, did she tell you what the carvings meant?"

It wasn't until his eyes narrowed that I recognized my mistake. "How did you know about that?"

"The sheriff showed me a photo," I lied.

His scowl grew deeper. "That's not the sort of thing a decent woman should be looking at. I'll have to have a word with him."

I held up both hands. "Please, I would hate for you to get into trouble over me."

"You're too sweet, Emma." He grinned at me in a way that made me want to shift. "I was wondering if you wanted to go out again this weekend. Dinner this time?"

I huffed out a breath. Damn it, I thought I'd made my position clear with the deputy. "I'm not sure I'm free. We have the blind date with a book event coming up and—"

"Let me know." His heart was in his eyes as he looked at me. Mother moon, how was I going to get out of this?

I made a big show of checking the time on my phone. "Oh man, I got to move it if I'll be back in time for dinner. See you later, Art."

Though my ribs screamed in protest, I jogged over the bridge and up the main street. The wind was picking up and the heavy look of the clouds indicated another snowstorm was brewing. My throat burned from the abuse. I was wheezing by the time I let myself in the kitchen door.

Hatty and Rue both glanced up. Hatty's gaze narrowed on me, and she asked, "What smells like barbecue?"

"Never mind that," I waved her off as I removed my jacket, then turned to face them. "Jody's estranged wife has been taken into custody. He had a million-dollar insurance policy taken out in her name."

The sisters exchanged a glance, and then Rue said, "I'm sorry to burst your bubble, sweetness, but she didn't do it."

"She didn't?" I plunked down into a kitchen chair. Without being asked, Rue slid a mug of mixed berry tea in front of me. "Are you sure?"

"Positive," Hatty nodded. "There's a message from a man on his digital voicemail and he threatened to, and this is a direct quote, "Carve him into bloody pieces if he didn't pay up."

The ghost appeared right outside my field of vision.

"It might be just a coincidence," I hedged.

"The man?" Hatty sounded smug as she added, "Used to be his partner on the podcast. He claimed the whole thing was his idea, and that Jody stole it from him."

"That," the ghost muttered. "Sounds like Wayne."

CHAPTER

TEN

Wayne, it turned out, was Wayne Vincent Tamarind. According to the Bramblewicks, he was a well-known podcaster, summoner, and legacy magical practitioner. Being a legacy meant that several generations of his family kept records like the ones Hatty had shown me. That meant Wayne knew about runes. Plus, he had one hell of a motive.

"Ten thousand dollars an episode?" I stared at Jody Haversham. "You're kidding me."

"Man, did I ever go into the wrong line of work," Hatty groused.

"So, did you steal his podcast idea?" I asked the ghost.

"No," he sounded offended that I even asked. "Supernatural podcasts are a dime a dozen. I did my homework though and did more than tell ghost stories

123

to scare people the way Wayne does. I've always been a research man."

I sat back in my chair as the timer beeped.

"That will be the pot roast," Rue chirped. "Let me get the potatoes on while you two get yourselves cleaned up."

It was clear she only meant me, as Hatty didn't smell like smoke and hospital disinfectant.

I pushed out of the chair and headed upstairs, Jody Haversham floating behind me.

"Can I get a few minutes to myself?" I snapped at the apparition.

He paused and then blinked. "I'm sorry, Emma."

"It's fine," I said, even though it wasn't fine. I was irritated and on the verge of telling him to piss off for good. His life had been a mess and every time I tried to help him, I ended up in over my head.

I slipped into the bathroom and then undressed. When my hand brushed the shower handle, Z's voice filled my mind.

Are you all right, petal?

I sighed. "Not really, but I'm too tired to get into it right now."

There was silence for a moment, but I sensed he was still there.

"Why didn't you tell me who you were?" I asked him. "You were starving, and you never said anything. Why?"

Partly out of shame. You've had enough taken from you, Emma. As his smoky voice filled my head, I found myself leaning into the shower wall. *I only wanted to make it better for you.*

That tracked with the altruistic streak I'd noticed. His comment about shame made me wonder if Z didn't like being a demon that fed on others. I would hate that kind of parasitic existence.

I swallowed and then turned on the hot water. Fifteen minutes later, I stood before the mirror, blow dryer in hand. I took stock. My hair was the same, not quite curly but not exactly a straight mess as usual. My body had that soft middle-aged look that no amount of dieting or exercise seemed to touch. Rounded belly and heavy thighs sans gap. Sagging breasts, creepy arm flab. Not exactly the form of a hero. My face and torso were a horrible mass of bruises and a few cuts from the broken window. The c-section scar had faded but was still an ugly, jagged reminder of the time before I'd come to Glimmer Ridge.

And that was just what was visible. I had fed an incubus infesting Glimmer Ridge with my sexual energy. A ghost of a dead podcaster that seemed to make enemies wherever he went waited for me down-stairs. A lonely deputy that I was using to meddle in a murder investigation and two elderly sister witches who wanted to teach me magic rounded out the roll call.

As much as I wanted to blame the ghost of Jody Haversham for ruining my life, I had to face facts. It had been wrecked long before he died. Z wasn't to blame for how he had to survive, and the only thing

Deputy Harding was guilty of was being clueless that I wasn't into him. The Bramblewicks were good-hearted souls who only wanted what was best for me. No one had forced me into that burning building, or to snoop on the sheriff's computer. That was all me.

The dryer was too much work. Instead, I clipped my hair up and then unplugged the hairdryer before heading downstairs. Rue was whipping the potatoes while Hatty set the table. "Anyone feel like a glass of wine?" Rue asked as she turned the mixer off.

I nodded, and Hatty took down the crystal wine goblets from the cabinet above the fridge.

We sat down together. By unspoken consent, none of us mentioned ghosts, murders, or witchcraft. Instead, we talked about the bookstore's blind date with a book event. It was the most popular Valentine's Day event in the village. That wasn't saying much. The cost was ten dollars a person and everyone left with a book from the used bin as well as one of Rue's infamous Death by Love and Chocolate chunk cookies.

After collecting the plates, I moved to the sink and turned on the tap. The water coming out was frigid. I silently counted to ten, but the temperature didn't yield. "Mother moon."

"What's wrong?" Rue paused from where she was transferring leftovers into a glass dish.

"No hot water," I huffed.

"Perfect." Hatty rubbed her gnarled hands together. "It's time you started learning the basics."

I stared at her. The only sound came from the

running water that drowned out my thoughts. "You mean magic?"

"No time like the present. Besides, magic works better when the wielder has true need of it. Some greedy witches will try to cast money charms when they aren't in true need. The universe always finds a way of striking a balance. Remember that."

I wanted to protest that I wasn't a witch, that as incredible as the Bramblewick Lair was, I really couldn't see myself dancing naked in the light of the full moon. It was freaking cold out there.

But the sisters looked so excited that I didn't have the heart to refuse. "What do I have to do?"

"Think of the elements," Rue said. "Fire mostly."

"I've had more than enough of that today," I grumbled.

"What?" Hatty's brows pulled down.

I shook my head and gestured for Rue to continue.

"Fire, water, air, and earth." Rue ticked them off on her stubby fingers as though listing ingredients for a recipe. "Different spells will call on different combinations of the elements. For hot water, you need fire and water."

"Or the number for a good plumber," I grumped.

"Emma," Hatty snapped.

"Fire and water," I repeated. "How do I conjure them?"

"You don't," Rue said. "You can't make something out of nothing. So, what you must do is harness the energy of what's already around you and channel it. Close your eyes."

Though I felt silly, I did as she instructed. The running of the tap filled the space between my heartbeats.

"Now, picture the colors you associate with each element. I use orange red for fire and bright blue for water. Pick whatever colors come to mind when you think of each element. It's important that you can visualize your end goal."

I recalled the curling black smoke as the fire consumed the ranch house. How it billowed toward me, a choking dark cloud. Water wasn't blue, it was clear. Colorless, reflecting the sky. Instead, I pictured the water vapor that surrounded Mist Glen.

"Look," Hatty whispered.

My lids lifted, and I stared at the steam rising from the faucet. "Wow."

"I've never been able to do that." Rue's tone was full of awe. "I can heat a basin of water or even a tub. But to change the temperature of the running water... Emma, you're a natural!"

Her delight made me smile as I reached for the sponge. "So that's all there is to it?"

"Not exactly." Hatty snagged a dishtowel and took the freshly scrubbed plate from my hands. "Everything has a different combination of the elements. Something like hot water is easy compared to healing a wound."

I thought about the carvings on Jody Haversham's corpse. "Do runes help find that balance?"

"Some can. Others will focus energy where the practitioner wants it to go, or can even transfer energy, like a conduit between two points that aren't connected."

I considered her words, then asked, "Do you think that Wayne Tamarind could have used runes to take something after Jody Haversham was already dead?"

Rue and Hatty exchanged a glance. "Not that we know," Rue said finally. "Then again, we don't work with death magic."

"Do you know anyone who does?" I asked, not daring to hope.

"Perhaps," Hatty murmured, gaze growing distant.

"Hatty, no," Rue was glaring at her sister. "He's not sane."

"Who are we talking about?" I glanced between the sisters.

"A witch. He used to be a member of our coven. But he doesn't play well with others," Rue gave her sister a fierce glare. "Don't we have enough problems without inviting Draven into the mix?"

"What do you suggest, Rue? That we send Emma untried up against Wayne Tamarind with no evidence?" Hatty raised a sardonic eyebrow. "He'll eviscerate her."

My arms went around my midsection.

Hatty noticed and flinched. "Sorry sweets, I didn't think."

I looked between the Bramblewick sisters. "You don't have to—"

"Fine," Rue held up her hands in defeat before jabbing a finger at her sister. "Just do yourself and everyone who loves you a favor and keep your clothes on this time."

"Do I want to know what that was about?" I followed Hatty as she stormed through the bookstore, down the dark hall and into her bedroom. I'd only been in the space a handful of times over the years. Hatty's room was her sanctuary when "the sheer stupidity of people got to be too much."

She rolled her eyes as she beelined over to her computer. "Rue didn't knock."

I blew air out between my teeth and considered what exactly Rue could have walked in on. *Nope, don't want that mental picture.* Yet it seared itself into my gray matter. Figured that I couldn't recall the memories I was desperate to remember and cursed with ones that would forever haunt me.

Hatty's room had been divided into sections. Her narrow bed was pushed up against the far wall and covered with a pretty patchwork quilt. An oversized leather armchair sat adjacent to the window with a reading lamp standing sentinel behind. A small folding table held a book and provided a convenient landing zone for a beverage. Her antique dresser gave me pause. It was strewn with all sorts of pill bottles. I picked one up and read the label, having no idea what it was for.

"Hatty?" I whispered.

She glanced over and then back to her screen. "Been meaning to clear that off. Never mind. Go sit where you'll be visible on camera."

Most of the space was devoted to Hatty's computers. The U-shaped desk held three enormous monitors as well as a PC that Hatty had put together herself.

Afraid to touch the thing in case my odd spiritual energy made it crash, I minced to the armchair and sat. From my vantage point, I could see all three screens well enough. Mage emerged from under the bed and began purring as he rubbed against my legs. The cat jumped up into my lap, claiming me. I stroked his orange fur. My gaze slid to the quagmire of medicine and then away.

Hatty put a headset on and flicked on the screens. The one on the left held what looked like a video game with a lush green jungle and a buxom warrior woman with purple-streaked hair pulled up in a high ponytail. The one on the right showed nothing but code.

It was the middle screen that Hatty focused on. I heard a ringing and then the blank screen was replaced with the image of a dark-haired man with graying temple streaks and eyes the color of obsidian. He looked a few years younger than me. His grin transformed him from average-looking to devilishly handsome. A Cajun accent floated from the speakers as he drawled, "Well hello, *cher*."

"Draven," Hatty greeted him in a warm tone rarely heard from her unless it was directed at me or Rue. My jaw dropped. *That* was the man that Hatty had been cavorting with naked? Then again, considering my odd relationship with Z, I had no room to judge.

"And who is that with you?" He asked.

"Emma Bishop, my cousin." Hatty answered.

I held up a hand. "It's, uh, nice to meet you?" Shoot, I didn't mean for that to come out like a question.

My shock disappeared a moment later when Hatty asked, "Is your granddad around?"

"I'll get him, you." The handsome guy winked and then rose. Hatty swiveled in her seat to face me.

"Draven is a family name," she explained. "The first son of every generation carries it."

I held up my hands. "None of my business."

"Damn straight." Hatty sniffed and then swiveled back when a white-haired man with the same prominent nose as his grandson sat down before the camera. "There you are, you randy old goat. Out chasing skirts? Better be careful you don't break a hip."

"Oh *cher*, you wound me." The elder Draven's accent was much thicker, the glimmer in his dark eyes just as lustful. "You know you're the only woman for me. Once a man's had the best, he wants nothing from the rest, for true."

"Spare me." Hatty rolled her eyes, but I could tell his effusive compliment pleased her. "Listen, I've come across something I don't recognize, and it seems like it might be in your wheelhouse."

"Send it to me."

Hatty opened the zip file full of photos I'd taken that depicted the swirling cuts and attached them to an email. A moment later, the image appeared in place of the jungle explorer. Draven, the elder, pulled a narrow pair of glasses from his pocket and perched them on the end of his large nose.

"I've never come across anything like this," Hatty admitted. "No one in our coven has. Normally power draining runes are administered before death. And these patterns make no sense."

Draven's bushy eyebrows pulled together. I heard him turn and mumble something in what I thought was French, and a moment later, the younger Draven appeared at his shoulder.

"This is nonsense." Grandpa Draven pronounced. A moment later, the Dravens were replaced by a magnification of the rune picture and zoomed in to a part marked with a digital red box. "See here how the circular patterns interconnect? That would nullify any magic draws."

"Then why would someone carve it into flesh?" I asked.

The blow-up faded out and was replaced by the men. Two sets of intense dark eyes focused on me as the younger Draven crooned, "I have no idea, *cher*, but that sigil isn't mystical. If I were to guess? It was someone playing with magic who didn't know what they were doing."

Hatty thanked the men and then shut off the camera. "That doesn't sound like Wayne Tamarind. He would have used the proper symbols."

My mind raced. "Unless he wanted to throw suspicion off himself?"

Hatty leaned back in her chair, arms folded. "That's a hell of a lot of work to go through to lay a false trail. Better not to carve the body at all. No, my gut is telling me this is a rank amateur's work. Someone who thought they could benefit from Jody Haversham's death but didn't know their craft."

I petted the cat and stared out the window. A light snow began to fall. "The wife?"

Hatty shrugged. "Perhaps. Or perhaps the answer is in one of those notes on his hard drive. It's going to take a while to sort through." She sounded tired.

"What can I do to help?"

She inhaled deeply and closed her eyes. "Let Rue and I teach you magic. We'll both feel better if you know the basics."

"Okay." I rose and Mage leapt from my lap and darted around the corner, tail

in the air as though he were flipping me off. Shaking my head, I made my way to the door.

"Emma," Hatty murmured.

I paused at the threshold and turned to look at her.

"You're doing the right thing." She smiled.

I quirked a brow. "I thought you wanted me to keep a low profile?"

"That was for your protection and safety. You're much stronger than when you first came to us five years ago. Able to stand up for yourself and others. I'm proud of you."

Her words warmed my heart. "Thank you, Hatty. That means a lot coming from you."

Then I headed upstairs.

I could feel him the second I entered my room and sat on the bed. My hand drifted to the wall. "Z?"

What happened to you today? I felt your fear, your panic.

I let out a long breath. "I saved someone who might have killed her husband."

He didn't say anything for a minute, then, *Come to me, Emma. I need to see for myself that you're all right.*

My teeth sank into my lower lip. "I don't think I'm up to feeding you."

You don't need to. Not ever again if you don't want to. Let me hold you in my arms.

I couldn't deny myself his comfort, no matter how wrong it was to use him when he couldn't leave. I fell asleep, my hand on the wall, and let myself dream.

The air from the beach caressed my skin. In the distance, the sun appeared to sink into the ocean. The sky was on fire, reds, golds, oranges of every shade so bright they nearly blinded me.

"Emma," he breathed.

I turned and spotted him, another glorious force of

nature. He held out a hand, and I hesitated only a moment before taking it. Callouses scraped across my skin as he threaded our fingers together, then drew me in for a hug. The warmth of him seeped into my cold bones and he rocked me back and forth.

It should have felt awkward. He was a stranger, a naked stranger. But the feeling that filled me was contentment, even when he kissed the top of my head. "I hate that I can't protect you out there."

"I can look out for myself." The words sounded hollow. In the last week, I'd been in a car accident and a fire. Had learned Glimmer Ridge was really alive, and that my adopted family was witches who wanted to teach me magic. Who knew what would happen next?

Though it took effort, I pulled out of his arms. "Is there any way to free you?"

"There is." I could tell by the way he glanced back toward the setting sun that he didn't want to tell me how to go about it.

"Let me guess, it's sexual in nature?"

His lids lowered over his light green irises until I could barely make out the color. "If I take in enough sustenance, I might be able to break free of this place and return to my body."

"Return...?" I shook my head. "You mean you aren't really here?"

"Neither of us are here, petal. At least not our whole selves. This place, this is the astral plane, the one that lies between your world and the world beyond. When you dream, your body stays where you leave it, and you project your awareness elsewhere. It's called astral projection. That's why your injuries are visible, but I'm willing to bet they don't hurt."

He was right. The ribs I'd cracked didn't ache here, the bruises no longer throbbed. "Z—,"

He placed his finger over my lips. That I could feel. It sent a spark of want through me even as he murmured, "Shhh, don't think about it now. I brought you here to ease your mind. Come lie on the sand and watch the stars come out."

He was the first to lie back. After a moment, I followed him down. The sun had dipped below the horizon, and the sky faded into the blue-black cloak of night. He began to sing that same song he'd sung to me before. His voice carried a resonance and power that filled my mind with music and blotted out all the fear, the pain, the anxiety that resided in my soul.

I wasn't sure which of us moved, but eventually, my head found the notch on his shoulder to rest. His arm curled around me as he lulled me to sleep.

CHAPTER

ELEVEN

"So let's start with your sigil," Rue said the next morning. We were back in the mystical basement the Bramblewicks referred to as the Lair. "The first thing you want to do is create a protection sigil. It's sort of like your witchy trademark. You can draw it, carve it, or simply imagine it and it will help protect you and reflect any negative energies into the ether."

Rue took a small notebook from her apron pocket and then drew what looked like an upside-down B and then a sideways R. She decorated the letters with snaking vines and leaves and then turned the pad around so I could study it. "This is my sigil. I draw it in the batter of everything I bake. I like to think of it as a way of watching over those who consume my food."

I smiled. "No wonder everything you make tastes so good. So, how do you go about creating one?"

"Sit down on the cushion there." Rue pointed to an

oversized pillow near one point of the pentagram. I lowered myself onto it as she retrieved a white pillar candle and carried it on a glass dish to sit on the stone floor before me, right in the center of the perfectly shaped star symbol.

"Clear your mind. First, you must empty your head of all your thoughts and feelings. Feed them into the fire. Then you'll be ready to begin."

I stared at her earnest face before dropping my gaze to the candle. Drawing in a deep breath, I watched the flame. It didn't flicker. There were no visible vents or ways for the air to get to the fire, so it remained steady.

What did Rue mean about feeding my feelings to the flame? Fire consumed and transformed, but it didn't take away the things that were a part of a person. Instead, I stared at the steady flame and let go of the sense of urgency I carried. The sense that I ought to be doing something, looking for someone. It was so much a part of me that I could barely manage to separate myself from those ingrained impulses. Somehow, though, I pulled the threads that bound me loose one by one and imagined dropping them into the fire.

The candle flickered as if I really had fed it.

"Good," Rue murmured. She set the notepad down on my knee and offered me a pencil. "Now draw."

My attention fell to the blank paper. I placed the pencil lead against it. My hand drew a sideways figure eight. In the center I drew two triangles, touching at the very tips, that looked like two dragon heads facing off against one another. I went over the design once, twice, and a third time. I wasn't pressing any harder with the lead or trying to stay within the original line. The shape grew smokier as I traced it for a sixth, and then finally a seventh time, before putting the pencil beside my thigh. I studied it for a long moment before offering it to Rue. She'd gone pale and her hand shook as she reached for the pad.

"Ouroboros," she breathed. "Mother Moon, preserve us."

"Did I do something wrong?" I whispered the question.

She shook her head and then forced a smile. "No, sweets. You did everything exactly right. Most people use their initials. It makes sense that you didn't, since you can't recall the name you were born with. This symbol means infinity or endless. A traditional Ouroboros is a snake or sometimes a dragon eating its own tail. But this," she pointed to the smoky lines, the heads facing off, and muttered, "I'm not sure why, but I get the feeling this infinity symbol is a fierce guardian. And you used the mystical number seven as an added layer of protection. Do you know why?"

I shrugged, uncomfortable with explaining what I'd done. "It just...felt right."

Rue blew out a breath and then ripped the page free along with her own. She collected a pewter plate and then tipped the edge of her paper into the candle flame. The fire surged once more and the edges of her paper blackened as it burned. She dropped the flaming piece of paper in the dish and then lifted her gaze to me. "When you feel ready, you need to burn it."

I waited until her paper was nothing but ash before I crawled forward and held the paper above the candle. The center of the figure eight, the triangle heads, glowed brightly before the fire began consuming the image. We waited in silence until the flame flickered out and only ash remained.

"Excellent," Rue beamed. "Now, go bury the remnants in the garden bed before your company arrives."

"Company?" I frowned. "Who are we talking about?"

She blinked owlishly at me. "You told me you were having a girl's night with Sissy."

Oops, I'd forgotten. "Oh man, thanks for the reminder."

"Anytime, sweets." Rue bent low and blew out the candle while I collected the ashes and we both headed up the stairs and out into the night.

The sun had dipped below the western hills, kissing their outlines in gold. The day had stayed above freezing, but just barely. I retrieved the trowel from the potting bench in the laundry room and then returned to the garden to dig.

Other than the weirdness with the Ouroboros, it had been a normal day at *Pages & Potions*. No ghosts, no voices calling for me. I'd wrapped all the books for the blind date event, enjoying coming up with quirky little descriptions for the tomes within. And I'd thought about Z.

It wasn't fair for the incubus to remain trapped in the house. I was going to have to feed him enough so he could break free of Glimmer Ridge. Selfish though it might be, I just wasn't ready to let him go yet.

Plus, what if he got me pregnant? Was that even possible when talking about an astral projection? How on earth would I explain that to Hatty and Rue?

Blowing out a breath, I decided the hole was deep enough, and I tipped the ashes into it before filling it in with soil and patting it down. I always wondered why both Hatty and Rue worked in the garden during the winter, but knowing next to nothing about plants, I'd thought they were burying bulbs.

"It could be worse," I muttered to myself. "It could be bodies."

"Do you always talk to yourself?" A snarky voice asked from behind me.

I jumped and then laughed when I spotted Sissy by the kitchen door. "You scared me."

"And what's this about burying bodies?" She raised a dark brow, blue eyes glinting with mischief.

"Inside joke." After dusting off my hands, I rose and then gestured toward the house. "Let's head in through the kitchen."

"Is it okay? Hatty's not going to come after me with a broom or anything, is she?"

"She hasn't done that in months," I teased.

We headed through the door just as Rue pulled a

batch of chocolate cheesecake brownies out of the oven.

"Those look positively sinful," Sissy breathed in deeply and added, "And they smell like an orgasm looking for a place to happen."

"Perfect for your girl's night." Rue set them on the counter to cool. "Just don't let Hatty catch a whiff. Doc Trammel wants her to lay off the sweets." Rue bussed my cheek before heading up the stairs.

"So," Sissy looked around the small kitchen. "This isn't exactly how I pictured it."

"What did you picture?" I asked before I cut into the brownies.

She shrugged. "Something more modern to match Hatty's laptop. I swear she could launch the space shuttle from that thing. This is nice, though. Very homey."

"I love it. Love the whole house." I turned my back before she could see my cringe and added, "Glimmer Ridge is a special place."

"Agreed. So, should we get down to it? I brought my DVD collection. We'll see what strikes your fancy."

I nodded and, picking up the brownies, we headed up the stairs to the television parlor.

Sissy set her oversized purse down and extracted DVD cases from the depths of the bag, along with a bottle of sweet red wine. I studied the titles with apprehension. I had a weird relationship with movies. Some I could remember vividly, even though I had no idea where I'd seen them or who I'd been with. They were like old friends who'd fallen out of touch. The experience always left me somewhat unsettled.

"What are we feeling?" Sissy asked as she fanned out the cases. "Super sexy or super sappy?"

"You pick," I said, unsure which was which.

She drummed her fingers on one movie case. "Okay, so I'm thinking we do a John Cusack fest. *Say Anything*, *High Fidelity*, and *Serendipity*. Sound good to you?"

"Okay." I didn't think I'd seen any of those, which meant none of my weird triggers.

We were halfway through the first movie, which I *had* seen and could almost recite the dialogue to when I noticed Sissy studying me. My hand flew to my mouth. "What? Do I have chocolate on my face or something?"

She shook her head, brows drawn down. "You're just different than I thought you'd be."

I blinked at her. "How so?"

"I don't know. You're...fun."

"Gee, thanks." I laid on the sarcasm.

She laughed. "I didn't mean it like you're boring or anything. You're always so quiet and sometimes it feels like you're somewhere else."

"Where would I be?" The question came out much hollower than I'd intended. Sissy was far too astute. I rose, trying to act casual as I headed to the door. "I'm in the mood for something salty. Popcorn?"

"Sure," she turned back to the movie as I escaped.

I leaned against the wall outside and shut my eyes.

Are you all right? Z asked.

No, no, I wasn't. I hated lying to people I cared about. And though I'd only known her a short time, Sissy had made her way onto the shortlist.

I let out a slow breath and then murmured to Z, "Yeah. I wish I didn't have to keep so many secrets, though."

You don't need to keep secrets from me, he crooned.

Anger flowed through me like molten lead. How dare he say that to me? For some reason, he wouldn't divulge. The incubus had decided to save my life and now I, a middle-aged, scarred, amnesiac, was his only option for nourishment, the only person he could talk to. Not to mention his only source of entertainment. Had he thought it was funny that I'd believed I'd been speaking to Glimmer Ridge for the last five years? Mother Moon, he'd made me come, and I'd cried all over him. Given a do-over, he would probably leave me to rot.

I made a disgusted noise directed at him as much as myself. "Oh sure, I'm going to open myself up to you when it's like pulling teeth to get an answer out of you. You didn't even tell me you were in trouble. That doesn't exactly inspire trust, pal."

I moved away from the wall before he could respond. He knew I'd come back. I wouldn't let him suffer forever. But to free him from his prison, I'd have to feed him enough energy to break loose from the astral plane. I'd have to reveal a part of myself that I couldn't remember sharing with anyone. And then he'd be off like a prom dress, back to seducing women by the gross.

Fucker.

If I were honest with myself, I wasn't angry at Z. I was jealous that he had a way back to his life while I remained stuck in place with no answers, a useless gift of seeing tagalongs, and no reprieve. Grumbling under my breath about the unfairness of the cosmos, I headed down the stairs and pushed into the kitchen. Hatty and Rue smiled at me, but their smiles melted away when they caught sight of my face.

"Is everything all right, Emma?" Hatty asked.

I opened my mouth, unsure what to say, when the house phone rang. I pivoted to pick it up even as I retrieved a bag of microwave popcorn from the cabinet above the toaster. "Hello?"

"Emma? It's me." Deputy Harding.

Perfect, just what I needed. I slammed the door to the microwave hard, even as I moderated my tone. "Hi, deputy. What's up?"

"I just wanted to give you a heads up." He sounded stressed, almost strung out. "The sheriff knows you were in the hospital in Gobbler's Ridge at the same time as Tanya Davis."

Shit. My eyes slid shut.

"I'm sure it's just a coincidence," he hurried on. "Something you can explain. But he's on his way over to your house to talk to you."

"Now?" I glanced at the clock. It was after nine.

"He said he would stop by after he finished up at the coroner's office."

"Coroner's office?" My knuckles turned white as I gripped the phone tighter. "What are you talking about?"

A chill skittered down my back. I turned and spotted Jody Haversham standing in the corner. Ghosts couldn't cry, but his expression was full of sorrow.

And I knew. "Tanya Davis is dead."

TWELVE

As the deputy had warned, the sheriff's car pulled up about ten minutes later. Wrapping myself in my heavy coat, I stepped outside to intercept him.

"I heard you wanted to talk to me," I said by way of greeting.

"You've corrupted my deputy, Emma," Mac Yates groused. "He never would have dreamed of calling a civilian in advance. Of course, he believes you can do no wrong."

"I didn't do anything," I began.

"Then why were you in the hospital with Tanya Davis over in Gobbler's Ridge yesterday?" He removed his hat and raised a brow.

I blew out a breath. "It's difficult to explain."

"Try." His tone was dry as dirt.

Letting out a slow breath, I tried to sum it up without revealing the ghost's part in what happened.

"Okay, bottom line, I went to her house. When I arrived, smoke was pouring out and I heard her call out for help. I tried calling 911 but had no cell service. So I went in and dragged her out."

"Just like that?" The sheriff appeared skeptical as he eyeballed me. Could I blame him, considering I'd had the same sort of thoughts about my abilities?

"It was just one of those things, like a grandmother lifting a car off a trapped child. Adrenaline, you know?" My shoulders bobbed up in a quick shrug.

"I do know. I also know you haven't given me a good reason to explain what you were doing at her house in the first place."

What could I say? If I told him I'd been there to offer condolences on her husband's passing, he'd want to know how I found out about her. So I kept my trap shut.

"Emma, I've got to tell you this doesn't look good," the sheriff grumbled. "I don't know what in thunder you're thinking by mixing in with this investigation, but you aren't doing yourself any favors. Two people are dead. Stay out of this case."

He turned, but before he could stride down the steps I blurted, "Was it murder, too? Like Mr. Haversham?"

The sheriff glanced at me over his shoulder. He didn't answer. I didn't need him to because, behind him, Jody Haversham's ghost nodded. He floated over to where I stood and together we watched the sheriff drive off.

"It was the same," Jody whispered.

I turned toward him. "Did you see who did it?"

He bobbed up and down, his feet a few inches off the porch even as he said, "No. I wasn't at the sheriff's office when she escaped custody."

My lips parted. "How...?"

He sighed. "Tanya had a record, Emma. She had served time for B&E. She was one of the best escape artists to ever live. All she needed was time to break out. Whoever killed her must have known that and waited for her."

Though my stomach twisted, I asked the question I needed to know the answer to. "The carvings?"

He bobbed up and down in ghostly affirmative.

I shivered and then turned back to the door. Hatty, Rue, and Sissy had congregated at the front of the store, all looking at me with expectant expressions.

"It was murder. The runes, all of it, just like Jody."

"Murder," Sissy breathed, her blue eyes huge in her pale face. "Why was he talking to you?"

"I met the victim." I didn't elaborate on the circumstances.

I turned to face her. "Maybe you should go."

She nodded, and I half expected her to flee, leaving nothing but dust in her wake. However, she took the time to reach out and put a hand on my shoulder. "If you want to talk, just call me."

She headed upstairs to collect her bag.

"Fire?" Rue whispered. Her nostrils flared as if she

could still smell the smoke that had clung to me when I arrived home.

"Wait." Hatty held up a hand and gestured toward the stairs.

Sissy reemerged, her hobo bag slung over one shoulder. She offered us a tight smile before slipping out the door. Hatty locked it behind her and then pressed her nose to the glass, making sure Sissy left. Once the Civic's headlights disappeared down the road, Hatty refocused on us.

"We need to call the coven. There's someone out there killing people and according to what Draven said, they might be intentionally trying to frame witches."

Rue licked her lips. "We still don't have a car."

"I'll ask Draven to pick us up tomorrow night. I want him there to weigh in on the markings..."

"It won't make Ursula happy," Rue cautioned. "You know they can't stand each other."

"I don't give a shit," Hatty snapped. "Mother Moon, this is a matter of life and death. And I'm not about to sit on the sidelines and wait for the modern-day witch hunts to kick off."

Rue wrung her hands. "Do you really think it will come to that?"

"Let's hope not." Hatty pulled her sister into a hug. "Go on now and call the coven. I'll contact Draven and set it up. And you, Emma," she turned toward me, and her lips compressed as though she'd changed her mind about what she'd been intending to say. "Go get some rest. We'll talk about the fire another time."

Relieved, I headed up the stairs. My mind churned over everything I'd learned. Jody Haversham waited by the door to my room. The ghost looked as though he had something more to say.

Something he said flitted through my mind. "Your wife was a witch, wasn't she?"

He thudded down to the ground. Well, as close as a ghost can come to thudding. "How...?"

"You said she was good with locks. That she could escape anything." Plus, I was in her house. It didn't occur to me at the time, but the cast iron pan I'd tossed through the window had been filled with a potion. I now recognized it as a protection spell. Rue made it under the light of the waxing moon when her anxiety got the best of her.

He nodded slowly. "I'm not sure if Tanya even knew what she was. It was what had me researching the occult to begin with. I was trying to find answers to help her. She was tormented, Emma. She thought she was crazy."

"I can relate," I sighed. "Just tell me one thing. Is her ghost going to show up here too?"

He shook his head. "No. I felt her cross over. She's finally at peace."

I blew out a breath and then nodded. "Okay, Jody. I need some rest. We'll see what we can find out about your former business partner tomorrow."

He wavered out of view, and I let myself into my

room. I could feel Z poised to speak, but he waited for me to make the first move.

After kicking off my shoes, I lay on my bed. I took a deep breath, shut my eyes, and then let my fingers trail over the wall.

The feel of the ocean breeze lifting my hair let me know I'd arrived. My eyes opened, and I surveyed the endless expanse of ocean. Night and day didn't sync up with the real world because it appeared to be mid-morning. "Z?"

"Here, Emma."

I turned to find him seated beneath a wavering palm tree. His hands were busy tying knots in a length of rope.

"What are you doing?" I asked.

He glanced at me briefly. "Making a hammock. I'm tired of having sand in places sand has no business being."

I coughed to cover my sudden laugh. He sounded so grumpy. "Can I help?"

He shook his head and then rose, standing before me in all his naked glory. My mouth went dry. I'd looked him over before, but I hadn't *seen* him. The incubus was perfect in body and face. All lean hard muscles, Slavic cheekbones, and those light green eyes that scorched me to my marrow.

I watched as he tied one of the longer ropes around the base of the palm tree and then tugged the hammock out. The braided netting stretched, hanging suspended between the trees. He pushed on it, muscles flexing with the motion. Then he flopped on it. The ropes creaked but held his weight easily. It swung back and forth in a gentle rocking rhythm.

I shifted on the sand, wondering how to reveal what I'd come here to say.

"So," he crooned, his gaze fixed on the palm fronds that swayed in the breeze. "Are you still angry with me?"

Figured he would bring that up. "I was never really angry with you."

"Liar," he crooned and tapped the side of his skull. "Remember, Emma. I sense your feelings. And you were having some strong ones focused in my direction earlier."

"The situation we're in is upsetting." I tried to reframe the problem. "I'm angry because I feel like neither of us has a choice."

"So you wish to be rid of me?" His head turned and those clear green eyes hooded as he drank me in. "Now that you know I'm not some innocent spirit of your beloved Glimmer Ridge?"

"What? No." Before I thought it through, I'd strode over to where he lay sprawled and indolent like a big lazy cat taking in the sun. "Are you mad at me about something, Z? Because it seems like you're trying really hard to pick a fight."

He sat up in a rush. "There's only one part of me that's really hard, petal. And there are better things to do than fight."

Before I could blink, he'd reversed our positions, so

I lay flat on my back, supported by the hammock. He towered over me. The sun was directly behind his head, obscuring his features until he looked like nothing more than a dark shadow.

I struggled to sit up. "Z, what are you doing?"

"You said you wanted to feed me. Well, you should know that I am *ravenous* for you."

His head dipped. Without conscious thought, I arched up, greedy for the kiss I knew was coming. Instead of claiming my mouth, however, those soft lips caressed my cheek. His ragged breaths feathered across my face as he whispered in my ear, "Emma, you have no idea what you do to me, do you?"

My brain clouded over with lust. I struggled to hold on to the thoughts that had been rolling around since the last time we'd touched.

"Stop it." I pulled back, struggling to right myself. "Don't say things you don't mean."

His dark brows drew together. "What don't I mean?"

Unable to look at him, I shut my eyes. "I'm all you've got. You were willing to let yourself die rather than let me help you. You can't truly want...me." That came out too self-pitying, but I couldn't call the words back.

"Emma," he breathed. Big hands cupped my face. "Love, look at me. I crave you with my every breath."

"Then why did you wait so long?" I whispered.

"I was trying to spare you the conflict. You aren't ready. You might never be ready. You're pushing yourself to give me more than you can for my sake. And... I'd never fed that way before." He glanced away, and I saw a muscle jump in his jaw.

"What?" I whispered. "Why not?"

"I had...other sources of nourishment. Ones that are no longer available to me. At the time, I thought it was better to subsist any other way than to give in to my incubus impulses."

My heart pounded as I began to understand what he was saying. Z hated what he was, how he had to survive. The demon hated what he was.

"I'm sorry," I breathed. "If I'm making this worse for you."

He raised my knuckles to his mouth and brushed a soft kiss over them. "Don't ever apologize for how you feel, petal."

"It's not fair to you, though." I shook my head.

"Life is seldom fair, love."

No shit. "You don't want me, though. I'm the only game in town." I couldn't keep the hurt out of my voice as the words emerged.

"Emma, look at me."

Against my better judgment, I did look up and held that sea-glass gaze.

"You are the most giving soul," he whispered. "The purest form of light that has ever existed. I am honored that you would share yourself with me, even if it's only out of some misplaced sense of obligation."

My lips parted to refute his claim. Did he honestly

believe I came to him only out of pity? But then he kissed me. The urge to argue vanished.

Mother Moon help me, Z could kiss. It started as a soft brushing of his full lips over mine. A message of adoration delivered with mouths and breath and the gentle sweep of his tongue as he cradled my face, holding me still to pay homage to me.

My hands lifted, needing more contact with his warm skin. My fingers curled over his biceps, and I tried to pull him down on top of me. He resisted with a dark chuckle that made me wet.

"As much as I loathe what I am, I adore that it can make you so senseless for me. I will feed because I don't wish to fight with you over my survival, petal. And because I'm a selfish bastard. I would do anything to touch you. But I vow that I won't take more than you are ready to give. So you're going to show me where the line is."

Before I could ask what he meant, he reached down to tug my sweater over my head. His lips trailed a hot series of kisses over my newly bared arms. Who would have ever thought the inside of an elbow was so sensitive?

Then his words registered—right as he sucked my middle and index finger between those lush lips. "What do you mean, show you?"

His grin turned wicked as he nipped the pads of my digits. His hands began unfastening my jeans. With one easy push, he propelled me farther back into the hammock. Clever fingers hooked in the waistband of my pants and with a deliberate tug, he tore denim and cotton underwear down my hips and off.

I lay before him a half-naked sacrifice. He released my fingers and guided the wet digits between my legs before he answered my question. "Exactly what I said. I want you to show me what gives you pleasure."

CHAPTER

THIRTEEN

O h no. No frigging way. The demon was out of his mind. It was one thing to throw myself into the flame he ignited inside me and lose myself in his hot touches until I climaxed. But what he was suggesting...that I touch myself in front of him...

My thighs reflexively clamped together, trapping our joined hands between them. Even that contact felt incredible.

"You're shaking," Z murmured. His free hand skimmed along my belly. "Even though I know you're as hungry as I am for your relief. Tell me why?"

"I can't." My head swung back and forth.

That maddening hand traveled up to cup my breasts through the thin cotton of my bra. It was about as unsexy as undergarments came, yet the way he looked at me made me feel as though I wore Victoria's Hottest Secret.

"Give me one good reason," Z cajoled in a voice that clearly stated there was no reason he would accept as good enough.

About a million responses flew through my head. *Because I don't know you, because I feel awkward and exposed under the bright sun.* But what left my lips was, "Because I can't come that way."

My answer surprised him. I knew by the way he blinked and then blinked again, as though something in his universe required realignment.

"Are you saying you don't touch yourself? That you haven't over the last five years?"

I swallowed and looked away.

His free hand caught my chin, forcing my gaze back to his. "Don't hide from me, petal."

"I have done that. But I can't...you know." I heaved a frustrated sigh and again tried to extract my hand from his grip. "So you're just going to have to think of something else."

He didn't relent. If anything, his jaw set at a stubborn angle and those green eyes narrowed to slits. "Let me help you with this."

I was about to tell him to go kick rocks, but then noticed something that changed everything. Z held his breath. As though my trusting him mattered. This was more than just a whim or a little side dish of kink for him. He truly did want to help me.

The words tore from my chest as though making a jailbreak. "I'll try."

"Good girl," he murmured. His hungry gaze was so full of approval that it made my sex clench.

"What," I had to clear my throat and then try again. "What do you want me to do?"

"Lie back. Relax," he instructed.

Easier said than done. But I reclined into the hammock. Took a deep breath as I stared up at the palm trees swaying in the sea breeze.

"Unclench your thighs, petal. Show me all of your lovely secrets."

Another shuddering breath escaped, and I forced my legs to part. They trembled as I separated them a few inches.

"Oh Emma," he sighed, as though he was beholding something wondrous. "You're lovely. So pink and puffy and slick. How could you not want to touch this lovely pussy?"

His words made me clench around nothing. From his vantage, kneeling before me in the sand, there was no way he could have missed it. The dark chuckle that emerged from him confirmed it even as he sucked my two fingers into his mouth, wetting them thoroughly before guiding them down to my spread-open sex.

"You're a flower in full bloom. Kissed with dew," he crooned.

If I hadn't known he was an incubus before that moment, the poetic way he was describing my body would have clued me in. Only a true sex demon could have sent such a thrill racing through my blood.

"Can you feel the heat coming from your core?" he murmured as he angled my hand directly over the opening to my body.

Wordlessly, I nodded.

"Dip your fingers inside. Feel how lush and ripe you are there." His hand remained in place, giving me the final say in when and where I explored. I wanted to do as he said, if only to ensure he'd keep saying those delicious things to me. My walls fluttered again, needing to be caressed and stroked in a way I'd never experienced.

My fingers dipped inside. A moan escaped as the slickness coated my fingers.

"Good girl," Z's hand glided up my leg as though praising me. "Where is the need greatest? Is it deep inside you?"

I did feel the urge there, but the temptation was higher, pulsing in time to every beat of my heart. "No."

"Show me, petal. Show me where you ache to be touched."

He barely had to urge me on. I'd grown so eager to stroke the pad of those wet fingers over my throbbing clit.

Z hummed in approval. He lifted the leg he held up and then draped it across his shoulder, scooting in even closer, until I could feel his hot breath on my slick flesh.

"Would you let me kiss you here, Emma? Just a gentle lick across that tender little bit you're hellbent on tormenting."

My back arched, and I gasped, "Yes."

But the tease didn't do anything more than chuckle darkly.

"I think I will, as a reward, after you come."

Panting, I turned and met his light green stare as I grated, "Tease."

"Temptress," he countered and kissed my inner thigh, sinking his teeth lightly into the flesh there, causing a groan to escape.

He wasn't going to help me. Fine. My lids slid shut as I explored, hunting for the rhythm that best pleased me. The magic code that would send me over the edge. More wetness seeped from my core. It was his turn to groan. My eyelids cracked open at the sound and I saw him lick his lips before meeting my gaze head-on.

Shock ripped through me at the hunger I saw in those light green irises. He wanted me. Not just the orgasm that would feed him. It pained him not to kiss me the way he wanted to, to lean forward and take my dripping wet sex into his mouth.

He was holding back...for me.

That thought was what finally sent me flying. My hand worked harder as I bucked into my own touch, letting the release wash through me like the way the tide washed up on the shore—relentlessly.

That shimmering gold mist emerged from my skin. I stared at it in wonder as it hovered over me, the proof of my pleasure fulfilled. And then Z leaned up. I felt the rise and fall of his shoulders as he drew a long, continuous inhale, pulling the shimmering energy into himself. His eyes slid shut in bliss as he took it all in.

My lips parted as I witnessed the effects. His muscles seemed to expand, his skin to shine with health. And when he opened his eyes, those peridot irises glowed out at me.

"Beautiful," I whispered.

"Yes, you are." His lids grew heavy as he looked down at my wet and well-petted sex. Before I could tell him that I'd meant him, he'd dipped down and sucked my wet fingers into his mouth.

I gasped as his tongue lashed out. It caressed along the side of my clit. My hand flew up into his dark hair, though I didn't know if I intended to push him away or draw him closer to me. His lips caught the throbbing bud and tugged so lightly I thought I would die from the pleasure.

It wouldn't have mattered either way. Z was a demon on a mission. His one objective? To eat me out better than I'd ever dreamed possible.

His tongue was wet, hot bliss as it slid through blood-engorged folds. His hands gripped the edge of the hammock as he slid down lower, and then his tongue speared into my opening.

I cried out at the sensation. He rocked the hammock back and then forward again, impaling me on his slick appendage. Thoughts scattered as he tongue-fucked me, using my suspended weight to go deeper on each push.

The orgasm stole over me in a hot, wet rush. Completely unprepared for it, I had no choice but to let it drag me under. Like a tidal wave, it crashed over the top of me, tearing me away from everything I'd ever known.

I must have blacked out at some point. When I finally lifted my lids, Z had adjusted my legs so that my weight was completely held by the hammock. Then he climbed in behind me, his front to my back. I murmured a protest. The man still hadn't come, but he soothed me with a murmured, "Sleep now, petal."

With a contented sigh, I drifted off in his arms.

THE DRAVENS PICKED us up in a massive Sedan that looked like some sort of military vehicle on steroids. The younger of the pair sat behind the wheel. His grandfather lounged on the bench seat behind him.

Hatty and Rue squabbled over the back seat and who would sit beside whom. The younger Draven clambered down and moved around the front of the vehicle so he could open the passenger side door for me. "Allow me, *cher*."

"Thanks," I said as he offered me a hand up.

"No, thank you." There was a twinkle in his dark eyes as he bent and kissed my hand.

I jumped at the surprising contact. He let go of me with a wink and then rounded the vehicle and slid behind the wheel. I tugged my gloves on for good measure. Even though I was only feeding Z, I was a one-man-at-a-time kind of woman. And after what we'd done on that beach the night before, I had no intention of flirting with Draven, no matter how charming or sexy the man might be.

"Is the fogy contingent finally settled?" Draven quipped as he buckled his seatbelt.

"Just drive the car, you whippersnapper." Hatty sniffed. I had to cover my mouth, so she didn't spot my grin.

Draven, the elder, and the Bramblewicks bickered all the way to the cemetery at Pine Hill, mostly about Wayne Tamarind.

"Can you believe they meet in a cemetery?" the younger Draven whispered. "That is the creepiest thing I ever heard, for true."

"Technically, it's a gazebo next to the cemetery," I murmured. "But I totally get what you mean. I usually stay in the car and wait." It was the best way to pretend I couldn't see or hear the ghosts.

Tagalongs congregated in certain places. Cemeteries, hospitals, and, for some odd reason, shopping malls were often their favorite haunts.

"You're welcome to pass the time with me, *cher*." He winked.

"Not this time, I'm afraid. I'm the reason for the

emergency meeting." At least my experience was what made them aware of the situation.

Draven, the elder, said something in French and his grandson responded in kind. I took the opportunity to practice the skill Rue had taught me that morning over breakfast—reading auras.

Rue's aura was a healthy and seemingly robust pink. Hatty's aura carried a sickly yellow tint over her natural brick red, which had me worried. Both the Draven's had dark blue auras, though in much different shades. Granddad Draven's aura was navy, while the younger man's resembled more of a cobalt color.

I couldn't see my own aura. Not even when I looked in the mirror. Rue assured me it was a beautiful pure gold that rippled over my skin. That sounded a lot like the mist that I'd been feeding to Z. Was my sexual release carving off bits of my aura to feed him? An orgasm was called the little death, after all.

"Auras can tell you a lot about a person," Rue said as I practiced tuning in to my second sight. "A sudden shift in a person's aura can mean a lie or concealment of the truth. A fading aura can mean illness, injury, or even just a deep level of exhaustion. A bright red flash around someone's head usually indicates fury. Yellow anywhere on the body can clue you in to their personal pain."

I'd wanted to ask her about Hatty's muddy aura, but the jingle of the bell over the door indicated a customer and the start of our workday.

"That's odd." Draven frowned in the rearview mirror.

"What?"

"It might be nothing. But I could have sworn someone was tailing us, for true."

I glanced out the rearview mirror. "What sort of car?"

"Dunno, you. They were too far back. It's probably nothing." Draven parked in the cemetery lot. The five of us scrambled out. Jody Haversham appeared by my side and together we crossed hallowed ground, leaving small tokens like jars of moon water, quartz, and pennies for the guardian spirits that roamed the cemetery.

Hatty marched ahead, spine stiff, head raised at a sharp angle. She certainly didn't appear sick. Again, I shifted to second sight. Like seeing ghosts, auras were easier to read at night. I had to wonder if maybe I was mistaking the color around Hatty. Auras did pulse and, as Rue had explained, changed often with a shift in a person's mood.

With my second sight engaged, I spotted them before I heard them. The congregation of witches. This was a large coven, many of the witches traveling miles to join together at the Pine Hill Cemetery once a month. Or twice if a special meeting had been called.

It was impossible to tell a witch on sight. Moles and birthmarks didn't indicate magic. Some witches were tall and thin, others busty, and still others well below the average height. Some dressed in a way that telegraphed their beliefs, others wore jeans and flannels like me. The Dravens were both sporting suits and ties, though the younger had left his jacket in the car.

No, there was no way to glance at a person and decide that he or she practiced magic. Just like it was impossible to look at a person to determine if they were capable of killing someone.

Hatty moved to the edge of the gazebo and the elder Draven rushed forward to offer her his hand. The disdain on Hatty's face as she looked down at it was clear, but she took it, allowing him to escort her into the meeting. Rue trailed after them, but I hesitated.

"You sure you want to do this?" The younger Draven asked. "It's not too late to book it back to the car and go for a cheeseburger, for true."

"As tempting as that sounds," I grinned, though it fell away fast. "I better see this through to the end."

But even as I strode up the stairs, a hand clamped over my arm. I stopped and stared up into the face of death.

"You," the man had a goatee and golden eyes that flicked over me with contempt. "What are you doing here?"

My heart pounded. "You know me?"

His lips curled back in a sneer as he gave me a slow once-over. "You shouldn't be alive."

My breathing grew uneven. I'd been to the coven meetings before but I'd never seen him. Who was he? And how did he know me?

Before I could ask, a blast of raw power knocked

me clear across the gazebo. My midsection hit the railing, knocking the wind out of me. My healing ribs sang in protest.

I had been wrong. Death wasn't the man with the gold eyes. It was the woman with the flaming red hair whose hands flared white as she gathered the killing blow.

FOURTEEN

S uddenly, young Draven appeared between my stunned self and the redhead. Black flames rose from both of his palms, flickering like a living thing. Every muscle was bunched as he faced off against my attacker.

"How dare you raise magic against my wife?" The man who'd recognized me snarled.

"You want her, red? You've got to go through me first, for true." Draven ignored the outraged man and refused to back down.

"Wayne, Imogen, enough!" An assertive female voice called from the other end of the gazebo—Ursula White, the high priestess's voice rang out as she added, "You've been invited here as a courtesy, but if another astral blast leaves either of you, I will have you barred for life!"

The redhead's glittering gaze fixed on me, but at least the glow of her hands faded as she straightened.

Only when she turned away did Draven's flames die down. He glanced at me over his shoulder and mouthed, "Are you okay?"

No, no, I wasn't. My heart had nearly pounded its way out of my chest. No one had ever attacked me before. At least, not that I could remember. Oh, I'd been yelled at and had doors slammed in my face, but Imogen had murder in her eyes.

And Wayne. Wayne Tamarind, aka Jody Haversham's former podcast partner. Even though we had never met, he *recognized* me.

Somehow, I doubted that he'd be willing to sit down over a scone and have a civilized conversation about our previous acquaintance. Mother Moon, I had never met anyone who recognized me before.

Figured he was probably a murderer.

Hatty and Rue made their way over to me, two sets of Bramblewick blue eyes wide as they studied my face.

"Are you hurt?" Rue fussed as she ran her hands an inch over my body.

"I'm fine." Then, looking up into Draven's face, I murmured, "Thanks to you."

"Get him out of here." The high priestess made her way over to where our little group stood. Ursula was in her mid-thirties. Her dark skin gleamed in the fairy lights strung around the gazebo, though her eyes were as full of fire as Draven's hands had been a moment ago.

Two sorcerers grabbed Draven by either arm. He

jerked away from the men and then lifted his chin. "Nice group you have here, *cher*." He made a show of brushing the wrinkles out of his shirt and then looked back at me. "I'll wait for you in the car, you."

Turning to Hatty, Ursula sighed. "What were you thinking bringing them here? Trouble always follows a Draven like a stray dog."

"I'm thinking there's someone out there that's framing witches. That includes the Dravens. I don't think it's fair of you to remove him when he wasn't the one who cast the first spell unprovoked." Hatty gave a pointed look at where Wayne and Imogen stood.

The priestess stepped closer and lowered her voice. "Wayne Tamarind is an authority on demonic magic in our region. When you called an all-hands coven meeting, I had to include him in case he knew something."

He knew something, all right. Something about me. Judging from the way both he and Imogen eyeballed me, it wasn't my favorite color.

Rue helped me limp to one of the benches on the far side of the gazebo and urged me to sit. I did so, not taking my gaze from the duo, who might be the key to unlocking my past.

Not to mention solving the murders of Jody Haversham and Tanya Davis.

The elder Draven sat beside me and patted my knee. "You sure you don't want to go wait in the car, *cher*? No one would blame you after that."

"No," I huffed and then murmured, "What exactly did she throw at

me?"

"An astral blast." I started and Draven, mistaking my astonishment for confusion, added. "It's energy manifested from another plane of existence, one separated from the physical world."

"It sure felt physical to me." I rubbed the shoulder where the blast had hit and winced.

Draven made a sympathetic sound. "It can be gathered by one who can astral project onto that plane and used in our world. Imogen is a powerful psychic. I'm not surprised she can do that."

"And Draven?" I asked. "What did he do?"

"Wielded fire from the underworld."

My lips parted to ask another question, but Ursula took her place in the center of the gazebo.

"Thank you all for coming." The high priestess spoke in her no-nonsense voice. "I was made aware of a troubling situation that could affect all of us. Hatty?"

Hatty stalked forward and explained about the murders and the carvings that had been done post-mortem. While she talked, I took the time to recover and to keep my gaze on Wayne. More specifically, my second sight. I spied a flare of white when he heard about Jody's death. Was that surprise? Or maybe guilt? I wished I was better at interpreting the shifts in auras.

"Who's doing this?" A young witch wearing a long-sleeved purple dress asked. "And why blame us?"

"We don't know." Ursula took over. "But I want to

launch our own investigation. Because if the public believes witches are behind these murders, we're all at risk."

The tension ratcheted higher and higher as people asked questions we didn't have answers for. Hatty mentioned Jody's podcast and the various threats. I saw Wayne stiffen when her hawklike blue glare landed on him, but he didn't speak.

"If there's nothing else." Ursula raised her hands above her head. "There's no use in speculating. Anyone who wishes to be part of the investigation, stay. The rest of you should get back to your lives. I'll send out a newsletter with information as soon as we have any updates."

Several witches rose and exited. Imogen and Wayne were among the first to descend the steps. I got to my feet, even as Rue tugged on my arm. "Emma?"

"They know me," I leaned in and whispered in her ear. "I need to talk to them."

"Sweetness, I don't think—"

I tugged free, but then Draven stopped me. "Here, take this at least." He handed over a vial full of pink liquid.

"What is that?"

"Invisibility potion. No one can see you with regular or second sight."

"How long does it last?"

He shrugged. "Ten minutes maybe."

"Thank you." I palmed the potion and then hurried down the steps. I paused when I spotted Imogen and

Wayne. They hadn't headed into the graveyard. Instead, they stood by a giant oak tree. From their body language, it appeared as if they were in the middle of an argument.

Popping the cork from the little bottle, I knocked back the contents. It tasted like liquid cotton candy. Warmth crept through my limbs. Though I could still see myself as I looked down at my flannel shirt, jeans, and boots, I didn't doubt that it had worked.

Careful not to step on any twigs lest I give myself away, I crept closer. Imogen's hands were in the air, and I caught the end of her exclamation. "...told me that bitch was dead."

"I can't explain it," Wayne shook his head. "I summoned the death demon Azrael myself! There's no way she should have left that clinic alive."

I forgot how to breathe. *Death demon. Clinic. Azrael.*

"She can ruin everything, Wayne," Imogen hissed. "Everything we've spent years working to achieve."

"You think I don't know that?" Wayne ran a hand through his graying hair. "We'll take care of her."

"When?" The redhead asked.

"In a few days. It was foolish enough of you to attack her so publicly. Now we need to be extra careful. I know where that bookstore is where she lives with those old crones. We'll sneak in at night, maybe stage a gas leak. Something that will look like an accident."

His plan sent chills up my spine. No doubt the man was capable of murder. He was plotting mine. For the second time. I took out my phone and set it to record.

While I couldn't take illegally obtained recordings to the police, it might be enough to prove to Ursula and the coven what Wayne and Imogen were doing.

Unfortunately, my hands shook so badly that I dropped the phone. It clattered to the sidewalk.

"What was that?" Imogen's head jerked around.

I held my breath as the two of them approached me. Wayne stopped a foot away. I shut my eyes, hoping the invisibility potion would last long enough for them to leave.

"Let's get out of here." Imogen tugged on his arm.

Wayne turned and I barely bit back a curse when his foot kicked my phone. I had no choice but to watch helplessly as he bent over the device and picked it up. At least it was locked. There was no way for him to tell that it was mine or that I stood right behind him.

Dismayed, I watched as he dropped it into his coat pocket. Then, collecting Imogen, he strode off into the night.

"What were you thinking?" Hatty asked for the thousandth time as we stumbled through the back door and into the kitchen. "You had no clue if that potion would even work! You could have been killed!"

"Hatty." Rue sounded exhausted. "Enough. What's done is done. We need to strengthen the wards. Maybe take the younger Draven up on his offer to act as a night guard for us."

I sank onto the kitchen chair. "There's an easier answer. I could leave."

"You will do no such thing," Hatty snapped. "Glimmer Ridge is your home. Where would you go?"

I didn't have an answer for her. "He's after me. If I leave, at least you and Rue will be safe."

"Emma, no." Rue put the kettle on and then reached for her jars of herbs. "We need to stick together."

"At least sleep on it," Hatty urged. I saw the fear in her eyes. "You're exhausted and not thinking clearly. Go on up. We'll talk about this more tomorrow."

I nodded. Not in agreement but because I didn't want to cause either of them any more distress. Jody Haversham waited in front of the stairs, but I sighed, "Not now."

He vanished.

Slowly, I trudged my way upstairs and let myself into my room. The second the door shut behind me, I heard his voice.

Come to me.

I shut my eyes and then sat on the bed. My mind had been whirling, going over all I'd learned. I still didn't know if Wayne had killed Jody or his wife, but I did know he'd already tried to kill me once.

With a demon.

Slowly, I lay back on the bed and touched the wall.

I could feel myself falling and wasn't surprised when strong hands caught me.

"Are you hurt?" Z asked. He tucked my hair behind my ear, his sea-glass green eyes scanning me for injury.

"Define hurt," I asked.

Both of his brows raised to his hairline. "Something to say, petal?"

"I just learned tonight that a sorcerer summoned a demon to kill me. Being a demon yourself, I can't help wondering if you know anything about that?"

His lids lowered. His chest rose and fell. "I can explain."

I jerked out of his arms and stormed across the beach. My belly felt like it was full of jagged glass. "Oh, by all means. I would fucking love it if somebody explained something to me for once!"

His dark head was bowed. I saw his shoulders shift as he drew deep breaths.

"Well?" I snapped. "You said you had another way to feed, one that you preferred before. You're not just an incubus, are you?"

Slowly, he shook his head. "Only half."

"And the other half?" I waited even as my brain screamed that it couldn't be true.

He looked up. "I'm trying to figure out where to begin."

"Maybe with your name," I snarled. "Z is short for Azrael, right?"

My heart cracked when he nodded.

"Tell me how we met, Azrael. Please. I need to know."

A muscle jumped in his jaw as he rose to his feet. Though I'd felt shy about looking at his naked body before, I was too riled up for modesty. My gaze snagged on that mark on his inner thigh. The brand.

"You've already figured it out." He swallowed, but I gave him credit for holding my gaze. "I was the death demon summoned to end your life."

FIFTEEN

If I could have buried myself in fabric so I wouldn't make accidental contact with Glimmer Ridge, I would have. As far as I was concerned, Azrael's betrayal was the final nail in the coffin of this chapter of my life.

My thoughts whirled as I packed my bag the next morning, ignoring his pleas anytime I brushed against a doorframe or the sink. He couldn't follow me. For that, I was grateful. It was beyond time that I stopped leaning on this place to keep me together in body and soul. If I left now, Hatty and Rue would be safe.

A pang of guilt washed through me at the thought of Azrael trapped on that beach forever. I ruthlessly tamped it down as I slung the duffel bag over my shoulder. He'd lied to me, used me to feed from, even knowing his betrayal would cut deeper than any I could remember.

The amount of my actual possessions fit neatly in a

small duffel with room to spare. *Mother Moon, I'm a parasite*, I thought with a final glance around the lovely room that had been mine for half a decade. A being that lived off others and gave nothing back.

Like a certain Incubus.

Using the edge of my sleeve so I didn't make direct contact with the doorknob, I slung the duffel over my shoulder and headed out into the hall. Skipping the eighth and third steps, which creaked, I wound my way through the darkened bookstore. It was early enough that the Bramblewicks wouldn't be up for a few hours. I set up the coffee and laid out the tea so Hatty and Rue wouldn't have to fuss. I glanced at the pile of wrapped books for the blind date with a book event, feeling a pang that I wouldn't get to see the reactions of the people when they discovered their newfound treasures.

On impulse, I cut a piece of brown butcher paper from the craft table in the children's area and then extracted the copy of *Peter Pan* from my duffel. I wrapped it carefully and then wrote, "For the most wonderful women I've ever known. Thank you for protecting me. Take care of each other. Love Emma."

I set the wrapped book on top of the stack and then strode to the front door. One final glance around the dark shapes that I'd come to know and love so well and then I reached for the knob.

Don't go, Azrael pleaded. *Please, Emma.*

My eyes slid shut. Could I condemn him to imprisonment and starvation? Maybe I should tell someone about him.

It's not safe out there, he added.

"It's not safe anywhere," I told him and then let myself out into the night.

I walked down the dark streets of the village. A chill wind blew my hair back from my face. Ducking my head, I stared at the ground. With no real destination in mind, I was going nowhere fast.

The ghost of Jody Haversham appeared in front of me. "Emma?"

I ignored him.

"Emma, wait. You can't leave."

Pausing, I glanced over at the apparition. "Dude, watch me."

"This isn't right," the ghost said.

No, it wasn't right. None of it. I crossed the hump-back bridge, staring down at the darkened stream that would wind its way downhill to the New River. Inevitable. It couldn't fight gravity or the laws of nature. That's what I felt like I'd been doing, battling fate. I continued up the darkened trail that was a shortcut out to the main road. I could probably hitchhike. Maybe go somewhere where it didn't get so miserably cold every winter.

"What if I told you I know why Wayne wanted to kill you?" Jody called out.

I slowed and then turned to assess the ghost. "Do you?"

He nodded. "Please, I promise I'll tell you if you go back to Glimmer Ridge."

"I could order you to tell me." I took a step closer to him, letting him see I would do it if he didn't divvy on his own.

Ghosts didn't need to breathe but Jody let out a sigh that seemed to come from the pit of his soul. "Fine, but please consider what I say. You are in great danger."

Me in danger? Must be Tuesday. I bit back the sarcastic words and then relented. "Jody, I know you can't feel it, but it's freezing out here. I'm not up to a long, drawn-out conversation exposed to the elements."

"Let's go to my old place. I know where Agnes hides the extra key."

"Agnes?"

"Mrs. Otis."

I blew out a breath. "Fine. But if I get arrested for breaking and entering, I'm going to command you into the belly of a whale like freaking Pinocchio."

The ghost led me up the drive to the rundown farm and then indicated the private entrance to his old apartment. On our movie date, I'd learned from Deputy Harding that his cousin and wife had reconciled, so I was fairly sure the apartment remained empty. After removing the key from the fake rock beside the garage, I climbed the open stairs and then let myself into the tidy little apartment.

The smell of fresh paint greeted me along with

welcomed warmth. I looked around the small space, taking in the gleaming breakfast bar with pendant lights. Edison bulbs flashed on when I flipped the switch. The place had a real modern industrial vibe, not something one would expect to find in a studio above a barn.

"This is nice." I smoothed my hand along the exposed pipes that led into the small bathroom. A clawfoot tub stood in the center of the space.

"Reasonable too. She only charged me two hundred a month. Utilities included."

My jaw dropped. "Seriously? That's like unheard of."

"Mrs. Otis isn't trying to get rich, just to make her social security check stretch. Plus, she likes having someone nearby. It makes her feel more secure. You should ask her about renting to you. If you can't stay at Glimmer Ridge, I mean."

I eyeballed the ghost. "Nice bait and switch but I'm only here long enough to thaw out and get the answers you promised about Wayne Tamarind."

Jody drifted back into the common area. I followed and perched on one of the chrome barstools.

"Wayne is what is known as a summoner. His specialty is summoning death demons and using them as assassins. He's the middle man that important people go to when they want someone to disappear."

My lips parted in shock. "You're saying someone *hired* him to take care of me?"

He nodded.

"And you knew about this?"

"It's what broke up our partnership. And my marriage. I was obsessed with finding evidence to bring what he was doing to light. My wife thought it was too dangerous. She told me I needed to give up on my quest or move out."

"So you moved out." I sighed and shook my head. "Did you find anything?"

Jody gave me a helpless look. "I can't remember."

The fading had already stolen those memories then. Wayne's business model was brilliant, honestly. Demons don't leave a trace of themselves behind. No footprints, no DNA. They derive energy from each kill, so they are eager to enter into contracts. And once a contract is signed, the demon won't stop until the target is dead.

Except somehow I survived.

As though he read my mind, the ghost murmured, "You're the only person I know who ever survived an attack."

My eyes slid shut. "Damn you, Jody. Why didn't you tell me this sooner?"

"I didn't know!" The apparition protested. "Emma, you've got to believe me. Until last night when I heard you telling the Bramblewicks that Wayne was after you, I had no idea you'd been on his list."

I let out a weary exhale. *Mother Moon, I had to go back to Glimmer Ridge and hear Azrael out. Either that or I'd have to hold Wayne Tamarind at gunpoint and force him to tell me who'd hired him.*

I must have spoken the words out loud because the apparition floated in my face. "Emma, you need to avoid Wayne Tamarind. He can't risk word getting out that you survived after he was paid to take you out. You're a threat to his whole business model. And he doesn't respond well to threats."

RUE JUMPED when I let myself in the back door. "Oh, Emma. You scared me."

"Sorry, Rue." After hanging my parka on the hook, I studied Hatty, who sat at the table sipping her coffee.

"Were you out making nice with Draven?" Rue nudged me as she removed cranberry orange muffins from the muffin tin. "He's very handsome, don't you think?"

"Draven?" I shook my head. "I didn't see him."

"Oh, he's in his other form," Hatty waved it off, her eyes fixed on my duffel. "What were you doing?"

I held her gaze until she swore long and loud, ending with, "Damn it, Emma—"

"Wayne summons demons to assassinate people," I blurted.

The muffin tin clattered to the floor as Rue's oven-mitt-covered hands flew to her face.

"How do you know this?" Hatty spoke in a low tone.

"Jody Haversham. He found out about it and was trying to bring Wayne to justice. He said I must have been a target. That's why Wayne and Imogen want me dead. My continued existence disrupts their business model."

"Oh sweetie," Rue moved toward me and hugged me with all her strength. "I'm so sorry."

After a moment, Hatty rose and then wrapped her arms around both of us. She didn't say a word, which was somehow worse than Rue's blubbering. It showed how shaken she was.

"I'm going to move into Jody's old apartment," I told the sisters.

"No," Hatty shook her head.

"Yes. I've already discussed it with Mrs. Otis. I'll still be here during the day, but I won't put you at risk at night."

Rue worried her lower lip, glanced at Hatty, and then murmured, "If that's what you want, then of course we'll support you."

I nodded. "Listen, I have something I need to take care of. Could you cover for me during the event?"

"Of course." Hatty's tight smile didn't reach her eyes. "You've already done all the work, anyway."

"Thanks." Picking up my bag, I headed back upstairs. The second the door was shut to my room, I leaned into it and felt myself falling...

Again, I was scooped into his arms. Azrael buried his face in my hair and breathed me in. "I thought I'd never see you again."

For a moment I let myself sink into his embrace, let it comfort me. Then I pulled back and met his gaze.

"I need to know what happened. That night."

He searched my features as though trying to memorize them. "I heard what you told the Bramblewicks. I don't know the name of the sorcerer who summoned me. I never did. But I was dispatched that night like many others before."

"I was your target," I breathed.

"Yes." He didn't waver as he held my gaze.

"Do you know what my name was?"

"That's not how it works. Demon assassins usually get something with the target's DNA—a strand of hair or a drop of blood. I knew you were a female, and that was all. So I set out to find you. And when I did, you were already dying in some poorly lit room, cut open and bloody." His voice shook, and he had to pause before continuing his story.

"I'd seen horrific things. But the image of you cut open like that, that someone could have been so cruel to leave you in such a state. I took one look at you and felt something inside me shatter. I realized how numb I'd become to human suffering. It was as though the haze of detachment got ripped away. I was raw and new once more. Then you opened your eyes and looked at me and whispered two words. "I'm ready.""

A tear slid down my face.

Azrael reached forward and wiped it away. "Somehow you knew what I was and why I'd come there."

"And you spared me?" I whispered.

His expression grew agonized. "No, petal. I was a death demon set on the trail of prey. I'd made a bargain. There was no way to save you, not as you were."

My brow furrowed, and I rasped, "I don't understand."

He took my icy hands in his. "I had to take that life from you before I could give you what you needed to survive. Emma, you can't remember anything before coming to Mist Glen because, in essence, you died that night."

"Oh." The word exploded from my chest in a massive exhale. "Oh, wow."

"Now, do you understand why I wanted you to let me die?" Azrael whispered. "I took your life from you. It was penance for what I had done to you."

"But you brought me back." More tears escaped as I took in his agonized expression. "What does this have to do with the brand on your leg?"

"It's the mark of the bargain I made with Death. To let you live, I had to give you all the power I'd collected as his minion."

"So I'm a Death Demon?" The question came out as a squeak.

"No, petal. You're mortal. An enhanced mortal, but human for all of your gifts." He cupped my face and I couldn't help but lean into the touch. "Is there any way you can forgive me?"

I let out a shuddering breath. "No. There's nothing to forgive. You saved my life."

"After I stole it," his forehead rested against mine.

I took a shuddering breath, breathing in the ozone and musk scent that was unique to him. "Yeah, I can't say I'm thrilled with that part. But what are the odds that any other death demon would have sacrificed what you did to bring me back?"

"They wouldn't. Hell, Emma, *I* never hesitated before. It never occurred to me to question whether the person I hunted deserved to die. I was a slave to my craving for power."

"And you gave it all up for me," I breathed and kissed him.

Azrael resisted for a moment, stepping back. "Emma?"

"I'm ready to help you get your power back," I said and then unbuttoned my shirt. "Make love to me, Azrael. Make love to me and be free."

SIXTEEN

With my certainty that I walked the right path came fierce boldness and hunger for him. Though I'd never imagined stripping down to my skin in front of a man—or a demon—even as an astral projection of myself. But Z had taken his time to coax me out of my shell, to convince me that it was me he wanted.

Finding out what he'd sacrificed for me was the icing on the cake.

Emboldened, I shucked my shirt and then reached around to unhook my bra.

"Emma," my incubus pleaded as he stared at my naked breasts. "You don't know how you tempt me. But I can't let you do this."

"Don't you want to be free?" I tipped my head to the side to study him. He appeared tense, as though he strangled his self-control on the end of a tight leash.

"Not what I meant," he rasped. "The temptation is to be inside you at last."

I smiled and then reached for him. My hand curled around the stiff length that was like heated steel wrapped in velvet. He let out a hoarse cry, and then his lips claimed mine. Soft, smooth, and so hungry. He lifted me off the sand. My legs wrapped around his trim waist. His hands cupped my ass as he carried me to the hammock. My bare back touched the ropes as that wicked tongue dipped into my mouth. Gripping his shoulders, I tried to pull him down on top of me. I craved the feeling of his weight on me, the sensation of him moving inside me. No matter what happened after, I needed to know what it would be like to be his lover.

He pulled back, and that light green gaze roved over my face. "Are you sure about this, Emma?"

I nodded and arched into him, craving the contact that heated my blood. "Please."

He pressed his forehead into mine, and his lids lowered. "I wish I could take you somewhere better than this."

"The place doesn't matter," I panted. "I just need you, Azrael."

A groan escaped even as he reached down to unfasten my jeans. "Say it again."

Breath exploded from my lungs as hot, hungry lips trailed across my chest. "I need you."

His shoulder-length dark hair rippled as he

breathed. "My name. I've dreamed of hearing you call for me, desire me."

Our gazes locked. "Azrael, make love to me."

In answer, he sucked one nipple into his mouth. The hot, wet heat made me squirm. His lips held it steady as his tongue darted out to stroke over the taut flesh. And then the tight scrape of his teeth had me crying out wordlessly.

By the time he moved to the other breast, I teetered on the verge of climax. He must have sensed it because he dipped a hand inside my open pants, hunting for the stiffened bit of flesh greedy for his attention. Two quick strokes and I detonated under him.

Gold glittering mist emerged from me. He inhaled in one deep breath, making his eyes glow.

"Again," he rasped, the fingers sliding down to gather the slickness that spilled from my core, before returning to pet my clit with soft, quick strokes.

I couldn't catch my breath as he worked my body over like a master musician playing the instrument he'd been born to wield. Another release tore through me. My eyes slid shut as I rode the wave of pleasure that rolled through my body.

I heard him inhale the energy even as I felt his hands removing my boots and my socks and then tugging my pants and underwear down. He rearranged me until the hammock held my full weight. This time, though, instead of kneeling before me, he stood between my spread legs. The thick ridge of his erection prodded at my entrance, teasing me open.

"Tell me to stop," he breathed.

Thick muscles strained with tension. I'd been feeding him well. Instinctively, I knew that my next orgasm would free him from this place.

Leaning up, I rubbed myself along his length even as my lips grazed his chest before lying back down. "I'm ready."

The green eyes slid shut as though my repeating the words I'd first spoken to him pained him. When his lids lifted, his expression was full of determination. He lined his cock up with my opening and then eased inside me.

I gasped at the sensation, the fullness and stretch, the heat of him. But what made me quake was the connection. The union went beyond the joining of flesh. My gaze locked on his as he moved deeper into my body. The pressure built as he surged inside me, and I cried out.

"Emma?" His brows pinched and I could tell he thought he'd hurt me.

At least until the golden shimmer emerged from my skin.

"Oh," he exhaled and then drew in that single continuous breath that fed on my energy. I half expected him to stop then, but he didn't. His green eyes blazed as he rasped, "Again, love. I need you to come for me again."

And then he surged in, bottoming out with the head of his shaft, kissing the mouth of my womb.

My nails sank into his forearms as he threaded his fingers through the netting and used the leverage to slide partway out of me before shoving deep inside. Again and again.

I lost track of the orgasms that crashed through me. And with each one, he became greedy for the next, and the one after that. Lust-drunk, I gave myself over to him completely. My muscles clenched around him, determined that at last, my incubus would have his release.

When it hit, I thought his spine would snap—he arched so hard. My name tore out of his throat in a hoarse shout as I milked him for every drop of his seed. I could feel him coming, finally, deep inside me.

All the strength went out of his legs. He collapsed atop me. For a moment I feared he would dump the hammock and both of us would end up on the sand in a heap.

"Was it enough?" I whispered as I stroked my hand through his pitch-black hair.

His green irises glittered as he appeared to stare through to the very heart of me. His chest rose as though he were drawing in a breath to speak. Masculine lips parted, but before he uttered a word, he...disappeared.

"What?" I blinked and glanced around. The sound of the waves lapped the shore. A soft breeze made gooseflesh rise on my sweat-damp skin. No sign of Azrael. I was alone on the beach.

Stunned, I rolled out of the hammock. It had worked. I'd set him free. That was the whole point, but I'd expected...I don't know what exactly I expected. More than a nut and run, that was for damn sure.

After gathering my clothes, I looked out over the sea. The vista stole my breath, even as my heart shattered.

Then, feeling used, I stepped back into my body.

THE BLIND DATE with a Book event was in full swing by the time I showered and headed down to the store. Hatty's shrewd gaze roved over my features, but she didn't say anything as I took my place behind the counter and started in on the backlog of orders. Rosehip, lavender, and hibiscus blends were our main tea sellers for the event. We served the light pink liquid in clear mugs, so it looked as though our customers drank love potions.

Valentine's Day. Ugh. It took effort for me to curl my lip in absolute disgust at the idea. Other people got flowers and chocolates. I'd had otherworldly sex with a being that had admitted he killed me. *Way to pick 'em, Emma. Who's next, Wayne Tamarind?*

No, I wasn't that foolish. Besides, the last thing I

wanted was to tangle with his wife and her astral blasts again.

Sissy appeared with a wrapped book and offered me a tentative smile. "Hey."

"Hey," I greeted her and then gestured to the pot of tea. "Thirsty?"

She shook her head. "Nah. Listen, do you think when you get a minute we could talk?"

It took a lot of effort to keep my tone light. "Sure, but it probably won't be until after closing. This event is always a biggie for the store."

If I thought my words would put her off, they didn't. "That's okay. I'm happy to hang out and scout the prospects. Speaking of which, who is that sexy thing sitting out on the porch?"

I craned my neck to see outside, but I guessed who she meant. "That's Draven. His granddad is a friend of Hatty's."

"He's scrumptious," Sissy's eyes glittered. "Think he can live up to this enemies-to-lovers grumpy-sunshine romance I picked up?"

"It's always better in the books." The lie fell from my lips. However, it wasn't a lie because even if the sex had been out of this world—literally—I wasn't slated for the happily ever after romance novels always delivered.

Sissy waited while I rang up a few other customers. I was trying to figure out what to say to her about the other night when Mrs. Otis approached with a wrapped book.

"I'm so happy you're moving in, Emma, dear. My nearest neighbor is a mile away. Hank and I get mighty lonely out on the farm."

At least with her, I didn't have to force the smile. "Looking forward to it, Mrs. Otis. I'll bring my stuff by later."

"Oh, dear, it's Valentine's Day. Don't you have plans?"

"Nope, I'm as single as they come." I forced a smile.

"Pity," she said.

I took the book from her. "An amateur sleuth cozy mystery with a mother-daughter private investigation team. Hijinx ensue." That was one of my favorite descriptions. "I hope you'll like this one. This author is one of my favorite finds of the year."

"It sounds so good. I'm going to rush right home and start reading." She winked at me and then put her book in her bag and headed for the door. Broad shoulders and dark hair filled the doorway, though Draven stepped aside to let the older lady pass.

"My, you're a handsome devil." Mrs. Otis took her time perusing Draven's body like she would eye a used car, hunting for hidden flaws. "You married?"

His lips pressed together, and I could tell he was doing his best not to laugh. "No, ma'am. I'm not, for true."

Then, to my mortification, she turned and announced loudly so the whole store was sure to hear, "He's not married, Emma. You could do worse!"

Mother Moon. My face flamed. Apparently, my new

landlady was going to be as big a matchmaking pain in my ass as Rue. Fabulous.

Draven approached me, amusement glinting in his dark gaze. "Should I ask what that was all about, *cher*?"

"I would be eternally grateful if you didn't." Then, deciding a quick change of subject was in order, asked, "Any sign of our friends?"

"Not a whiff. I've been circling the place for hours."

Lowering my voice, I stepped forward and whispered, "Hatty did say something about you having another form."

He shrugged, but before I could ask what that meant, he spoke. "Listen, I need to take off for a few hours, check in with work. Will you be all right?"

I nodded. "We'll be fine. I'm leaving as soon as the shop closes. And gossip spreads like a rash around this town."

His head cocked to the side in an odd, birdlike gesture. "Are you sure that's wise, you? There are protection runes in place here."

"A rune won't stop someone from lobbing a Molotov cocktail through the window. I won't risk Hatty and Rue."

"If you're sure. Just be safe." He turned toward the door.

"Wait." Gripping his arm, I swiped a wrapped package off the pile and handed it to him. "Everyone gets a book today."

Bemused, he glanced down and read. "A black cat

x Golden Retriever Reverse Age-gap first in a supernatural series. You trying to tell me something, *cher*?"

Another blush stained my cheeks. "Just trust me. I have a knack for picking the book people need."

He saluted, and I watched as he headed out the door and down to the walkway.

"Hate to see him go but love to watch him walk away," Sissy sighed. "Can I assume you've got dibs there?"

I shook my head and moved to wipe up some crumbs on the counter. "Just friends. Honestly, I'm not ready for another relationship."

Her eyebrow cocked. "Another?"

Shit, I hadn't meant to say that. Before I could explain, the bell over the front door jingled again. Rue emerged from the kitchen carrying a plate of Death by Love and Chocolate chunk cookies. Hatty rose and came to stand by my side.

"What?" I scowled, glancing from Sheriff Yates to Deputy Harding and back. My stomach lurched. This wasn't a casual visit. For one thing, they were both in uniform and their expressions were grim. "What's going on?"

"Emma, we need you to come with us." The sheriff extracted a pair of handcuffs from his back pocket and moved to trap me behind the counter. I backed away from him with my hands raised.

"What is this?" Hatty snapped.

Deputy Harding circled the other end of the counter, trapping me between them. "Don't fight it,

Emma," he murmured as he tugged my hands behind my back and used another set of cuffs to bind me.

"I demand to know what she's being charged with," Hatty barked.

"The murder of Imogen Tamarind," the sheriff handed Hatty a paper.

All the color drained from Hatty's face even as Mac Yates continued, "Witnesses told us the two fought very publicly last night, even coming to blows. And Emma's phone was discovered on the body. Read Emma her rights." The last bit was directed at the deputy.

"You have the right to remain silent." Art Harding began to lead me out of the shop.

"Don't worry, Emma. We'll get you a lawyer." Rue called out as the deputy walked me out of Glimmer Ridge and into the Valentine's Day rain.

SEVENTEEN

M y back literally pressed against the wall as I sat on the cot in the holding cell, waiting for the lawyer Hatty and Rue had promised me. My head was a mess of thoughts. Imogen was dead—and from the snatches of conversation that carried into my cell through the air ducts, the sheriff suspected I was responsible for Jody and his wife's deaths as well.

Deputy Harding smiled as he brought me dinner of a cup of noodles and a sad-looking tuna sandwich on worthless white bread. "Sorry about this, Emma. We don't have the best menu selection around here."

"Art, you know I didn't do this." Ignoring the tray he slid through the slot by my feet, I wrapped my hands around the steel bars.

"It doesn't look good." The deputy shook his head. "We've got half a dozen witnesses that said you and the dead woman fought. Though they aren't what I'd call reliable witnesses. What were you thinking, hanging around those sorts of people?"

It was easier to look away than to deal with the judgment on his face. He wasn't wrong. The coven had thrown me to the wolves. So much for sticking together.

I bent down and took the cup of soup back to my cot. It was way too salty, but at least it was hot. I ate all of it and then huddled with my arms wrapped around my knees.

A tear tracked down my cheek. *Some Valentine's Day.*

The cold seemed to emanate from inside my bones. I felt brittle all over, as though I would shatter like glass. Jody Haversham appeared briefly, promising me that help was on the way. My glare had him vanishing before I could tell him to leave.

Damn it, if I hadn't let the ghost stop me, I would be halfway across Tennessee by now. Of course, I didn't have an alibi for the time of Imogen's death. No one had seen me that morning at *Pages & Potions*. I'd been with Azrael on the astral plane. But I couldn't tell them that.

I had another problem too. When we arrived at the office, the deputy had fingerprinted me. Those fingerprints would be put into the AFIS database, along with my mugshot. And whoever had hired Wayne Tamarind to off me might be notified that my death hadn't exactly stuck.

Would Wayne summon another death demon to take me out? Or would he want the honor of killing me himself since his wife was dead? No matter how many times I turned it around in my head, I couldn't figure out who could have killed Imogen. She'd been so powerful. I had an enormous bruise from the impact of her astral blast. She should have been able to fight off her killer.

Unless, of course, Wayne had killed her. Or summoned a demon to do it. Wasn't that one of the rules about murder, that the significant other was usually behind it? I wouldn't put it past the evil bastard. But if he had, why would he have planted my phone on her body? Wasn't it dangerous for me to be in the system and alert the person who'd hired him?

I must have fallen into a light doze because when I woke, it was to the sight of shadows creeping across my cell like tentacles reaching for me.

Rubbing my eyes, I watched as they snaked across the floor. Something about those dark, insubstantial tendrils felt oddly familiar. They snaked up the cot like a Cobra rising from a basket, swaying in time to music only they could hear. I didn't feel threatened though. Before I thought it through I reached out a single finger.

The moment the digit connected with the shadow, it pulled me out of my body.

Gasping, I stumbled and landed on my ass on the sand. Dark wings blocked out the sun. "What...?"

"Are you all right, petal?"

"Azrael." I breathed and stared up, trying to take in the scene before me. Unlike every other time I'd met him, he was dressed from head to toe in black leather. But it was those great batlike wings that I couldn't tear my gaze from.

Batlike, except for what looked like a curved talon on every point.

"Are you afraid of me now?" he asked as he tucked them away, as though embarrassed.

Silently, I shook my head. Then, "I'm more shocked that you're wearing clothes."

A delighted grin spread across his features. "Because you freed me, petal." He crouched down and his hand reached out to stroke my cheek. "I'm so sorry. I didn't intend to abandon you that way. Believe me, it wasn't by choice. And because I'm not ensconced in Glimmer Ridge any longer, I had to scour the astral plane for your energy signature. I couldn't find it until you slept."

My heart thundered in my chest. Oh, how I wanted to believe him. "Why did you come back here?"

"You're in trouble. I could sense it." He rose and then extended a hand and helped me to my feet. "We don't have too much time before my physical self hauls me back. Tell me what's happened."

I explained about the arrest and my phone being found on Imogen's body and ended with, "Do you think Wayne could be behind all these murders?"

"I wouldn't put it past him. Anyone foolish enough

to bargain with death demons is capable of anything. We need to hide you."

"Where?" I shook my head.

He hesitated. "There is a place I can take you where Wayne won't find you. The Hinterlands in the north. It's a rough existence, with none of the comforts you're used to. But you will be safe there. We'll need to go immediately."

"What about Hatty and Rue?" I whispered. "I can't just disappear on them."

His shoulders stiffened. "Emma, this is your freedom at stake. Perhaps your life."

"No, Azrael." I stepped back, out of his reach. "I've spent the last five years building a life. There's no way I'll abandon the people who have protected me. If anything happens to the Bramblewicks, I'll never forgive myself."

He let out an enormous sigh. "Petal, I won't be able to fight off a death demon if one comes for you. I don't have my abilities anymore."

"I understand." Reaching out, I stroked his cheek. His lids lowered, and he leaned into the touch. "Thank you for trying."

"Emma—" He reached for me, but I stepped out of the astral plane and back into my incarcerated body.

THE LAWYER ARRIVED at first light. I was brought handcuffed into the Sheriff's office. She rose from the chair as I crossed the threshold and waited as the cuffs were removed. She glowered at Deputy Harding until he withdrew, shutting the door behind him.

The top of her frizzy red-haired head only reached my shoulder. A round woman in her late thirties, she possessed sharp honey-colored eyes, apple cheeks, with a spattering of freckles, and a lush mouth. She looked more like a PTA mom than a criminal defense attorney.

"I'm Louellen Fraser. But you can call me Lou," she spoke with a Boston accent that went well with her no-nonsense demeanor. "I'm sorry I didn't get here sooner, but we've got a bail hearing set for ten."

"Okay." I let out a breath. "What are my chances?"

"Of making bail? Pretty good, even for a murder case. I'll argue that you have deep roots in the community and no means to disappear. The fact that you don't have as much as a speeding ticket will beef up our argument that this is just a case of the wrong place and time. Now, can you tell me what the fight was about?"

My teeth sank into my lower lip.

"Emma." Lou clicked her pen a few times before setting it down on her yellow legal pad. "The more you give me to work with, the stronger the case I can put together."

I shut my eyes and tried to figure out a way to thread the needle. "Imogen knew me from before I came to Mist Glen. I'm not sure why she had a problem with me, but if you ask anyone who was at the gathering last night, they'll tell you that she was the one who attacked me."

Lou's head bobbed as she wrote down what I said. "Okay, and where did you go after the gathering?"

"Home, with Hatty and Rue." At least that part didn't require any obfuscation. "And early this morning, I went to talk to Mrs. Otis about renting the apartment over her barn."

More scribbling, then Lou looked directly at me. "And at the time of the murder?"

"I don't know what time that was. I had a headache, so I went to lie down before the event." That sounded plausible.

"Any idea how the victim got hold of your cell?"

"I must have dropped it sometime after the meeting."

"Okay good. From what I can tell, there's no real evidence against you, just the eyewitness testimony that you fought with the victim and then left around the same time she did. Plus the phone that we can argue she picked up any time between when you fought and her time of death. With luck, we may be able to get the case dismissed on circumstantial evidence. Fingers crossed."

I let out a breath as Lou rose. "Thank you for taking on my case, Lou. I really appreciate it."

"Thank me when we get you free." She smiled and

dimples appeared. My lawyer had dimples. Mother Moon, where had Hatty and Rue found her?

Lou collected her notepad and pen and then strode with purpose out to the other room, passing Deputy Harding along the way.

"I need to use the facilities," I told him. Not a lie, though mostly what I wanted was to stall going back to the cell.

He led me to the small half bath. I eyeballed the uncovered window, but it wasn't much more than an arrow slit. A crow sat on the naked maple branch outside, its beady dark gaze fixed on me.

"Dude, is a little privacy too much to ask for?" I called.

The bird pivoted on the branch, turning its back to me.

That was...unexpected. Quickly, I peed and then washed my hands. I took stock of my face in the mirror. Winter pale as usual, though the sleepless nights and the bruises from the car wreck gave me a sickly yellow-green tinge. My not-quite-curly, not-quite-straight hair was a rat's nest tangle in need of deep conditioner and a comb. My blue eyes were bloodshot, and my expression appeared haunted.

How appropriate.

"Emma!" Deputy Harding rapped on the door.

I shot a withering look at the door and then drew in a deep breath before moving toward it. For no real reason, I glanced over my shoulder at the window and met the crow's gaze.

"Caw!" It screeched and then flapped off as though it had delivered its message.

A shiver stole over me. I swallowed my unease and then unlocked the door and focused on Art. "Time to go back in my cell?"

He shook his head. "You're free to go."

I blinked. "Say again?"

He nodded, though he didn't meet my gaze. "Judge called. The charges have been dropped."

Lou works fast. I would have to send her some of Rue's Death by Love of Chocolate Chunk Cookies as a thank you. She looked like a romantasy reader to me. I'd put together a care package the second I returned to *Pages & Potions*.

Art handed me my jacket. I wondered idly if I was supposed to walk back to the village when I spied Mrs. Otis's VW bus idling in the parking lot. Hatty waved frantically the second she spotted me. I hurried as fast as I dared, skidding in the icy parking lot.

"Hey," I said. "Thanks for picking me up. Though I don't know how you got here so fast."

"Lou called. Said you were good to go. And Mrs. Otis agreed to lend us the bus however long we needed it." Her smile was tight.

It should have been good news all around. Yet, apprehension filled my chest. "Hatty? Is something wrong?"

"It's Sissy," she managed.

Alarm filled me. "What about her? Is she okay? Has

Rue taken her to the hospital?" Was that why the other Bramblewick wasn't here?

"No, Emma. She's not in the hospital." She drew a deep breath and then looked me square in the eyes. "She's been kidnapped."

EIGHTEEN

The ringing in my ears wouldn't go away. Though I could hear Hatty talking, trying to explain that Sissy had left *Pages & Potions* determined to find me a lawyer. Lou had contacted them and said Sissy had hired her for me. Rue went to her place to thank her. The door was wide open and there were signs of a scuffle. And she found Wayne Tamarind's business card propped up against the sugar bowl.

"Why would she do that?" None of it made any sense. "And why would Wayne take her?"

Maybe because he couldn't get to me or the Bramblewicks. But I hadn't known Sissy that long. So why would the summoner have targeted her?

"Emma," Hatty exhaled wearily as she pulled up in front of Glimmer Ridge. "There's something you need to know. Something Rue and I haven't wanted to tell you."

"Okay," I spoke slowly. "There are things I don't know. Can they wait until we figure out a way to get her back safe?"

"We've waited too long already. Emma, when Rue and I did that reading on Sissy, we found out that your fates are intertwined."

"You told me that," I huffed with impatience. "Hatty, what—"

"They are intertwined because the two of you are related. Sisters."

I blinked, sure I'd misheard her. "That's not possible."

"It is." Hatty's lips trembled. "It's why Rue wanted you to spend time with her. She was hoping being with her would trigger your memories."

I shook my head slowly, unsure if I believed her. Right from the start I'd felt a connection to Sissy, a closeness. I thought it had just been two kindred spirits who connected in a small town. But what if it was the bond of family?

"It didn't though." Hatty's gaze turned soft. "Emma, I hate to say this, but we don't know how exactly Sissy fits into your past. What if the scene at the cottage was staged? What if she's helping him get to you?"

My instinct was to protest that the woman I knew wouldn't have done that. But could I really claim to know her when she'd kept the truth hidden from me?

Numbly, I exited the car and walked toward the kitchen door. Rue sat at the table gripping an earthenware mug. No steam rose from it, indicating her tea must have gone cold without her noticing. The elder Draven sat beside her, his expression grim. They both glanced up when I pushed through the door.

Rue's eyes shimmered with tears. "Emma, I'm so sorry we didn't tell you."

I held up a hand, not wanting to hear apologies at that moment.

Hatty removed her coat and then turned to face me. "What do you want to do, Emma? It's your call."

"We're going to get her back."

"How, *cher*?" The younger Draven emerged from the bookstore, pulling his shirt down as he moved, displaying his perfectly cut abs.

I didn't have the bandwidth for the oddness of him getting dressed in the middle of the shop. "Do you know where Wayne Tamarind lives?"

"*Oui*," The elder Draven nodded. "It's about an hour from here."

"Okay. Give me half an hour and then we'll head there." I held the younger Draven's gaze. "Just the two of us."

"What if it's a trap, Emma?" Rue called as I headed back out the kitchen door.

Pretending not to hear her, I shut the door and moved to the backyard. She didn't want the answer to that. An avid romance reader and the ultimate believer in the happily ever after, Rue didn't want to hear that I planned to trade myself to Wayne Tamarind. With any luck, I'd be able to distract the sorcerer long enough so Draven could get Sissy out.

Or I could take her out.

I had just unlocked the shed when someone gripped my shoulder. I whirled around and came face to face with Draven.

"Tell me the plan, you." He tipped his head in a way that looked oddly familiar. And birdlike.

A puzzle piece clicked into place. "It was you, outside the Sheriff's office. You're a crow?"

"Only sometimes, for true." He shrugged as if it was no biggie.

My lids slid shut. "Is there anyone who isn't keeping secrets from me?"

He made a scoffing sound. "Everyone keeps secrets, *cher*. The trick is to sort the ones that are personal from the ones that can get you killed, for true."

"You're very accepting of all this," I observed.

"Why fight who you are?" He raised a brow. "Now, tell me your plan."

It was rearranging itself in my head—the picture shifting to accommodate the crow. "I'm going to tempt Wayne to take me and let her go. If you stick close, you can get her out."

"And if she's in on it?" He breathed.

Though I didn't want to think about it, I murmured, "Then she's going down with him."

He let out a slow breath. "I'll meet you in the car, you."

Draven circled Glimmer Ridge, and I moved into the shed and headed down the mushroom stairway to the Lair.

After lighting a candle, I pulled out the book beside the one of death runes that Hatty had shown me. *Splitting Yourself, Astral Projection in the Modern Age*. I didn't have enough time to pore over it the way I wanted, but I skimmed the chapter on reaching the astral plane and detecting energy signatures. Then I lit a white pillar candle and sank with it to the center of the pentagram.

My eyes slid shut, and I concentrated on my breathing. I felt the separation of self, as though I'd become suddenly weightless. It was the first time I'd astrally projected onto the plane without having Azrael there to pull me to him. I floated up and up and up. When my lids lifted, I looked out over shrouds of creeping mist. Lights twinkled within the mist like multicolored stars. Auras from other travelers who projected onto this plane.

What if he wasn't asleep? He'd said he'd only been able to find me when I'd dozed. Would I be able to locate him if he was elsewhere? Shoving the doubt aside, I reached out with my mind and scoured the mists until I found the familiar energy signature. Breathing a sigh of relief, I followed it down to the being on the other end.

"Azrael," I breathed into his dreams, as I tugged the link. "I need your help. Meet me on our beach."

All it took was picturing the beach, the hammock,

the rolling waves of the incoming surf and I arrived there.

The sound of wings, the rush of air, and a shadow passed between me and the noonday sun. He landed and sand kicked up in a cloud by his heavy boots. Once again he was dressed all in black leather, the ankle-length duster cut to accommodate his wings.

"Petal?"

"I need your help." Could I trust him? We were going to find out.

"WELL, THAT'S EXACTLY AS EXPECTED." I peered out the windshield at the gothic mansion perched atop a hill. Leafless trees surrounded it, their naked branches making the place seem more threatening.

"Evil villain lair, for true." Draven cast me a sideways grin, but it fell away slightly. "You know what you're doing, you?"

"I haven't the foggiest," I breathed and then popped the door to the car.

Draven emerged and shucked his jacket. It wasn't until his hands went to his shirt and began to unfasten the buttons that I raised a brow.

"Shifting," he explained. My gaze darted away as he undressed, a furious blush stealing over my face. I couldn't help but glimpse the webwork of silver lines across his back.

"I'll leave the keys in the car in case you need to make a quick getaway."

"What about you?" It took every effort not to turn and face him.

"Wings, baby." There was a sound, and the air pressure shifted, making my ears pop. When I turned, in place of Draven, a large black bird stared at me. The caw of the crow filled the gloomy winter afternoon.

"Showoff," I muttered.

The wings flapped, and a feather drifted down to my feet as he took flight. I stooped down and plucked up the feather.

"Caw!" The crow shrieked as he perched on a Birch branch.

"We're going to talk about this when I get back," I told him. Then, pocketing the feather, I pushed past the wrought-iron gates that someone had very obviously left cracked large enough for a person. I barely even flinched when they slammed shut behind me.

I half expected Wayne to be waiting for me on the porch, his hand wrapped around Sissy's neck in menace. But there was no sign of him as I strode up the steps. The flutter of wings told me that Draven had moved from the tree to the eaves.

Raising my hand into a fist, I pounded on the front door. It creaked open the instant my knuckles contacted the wood. No, that wasn't unnerving at all.

Cautiously, I peered around into the darkened

foyer. A fluttering sound told me that Draven had snuck through the cracked door an instant before it too slammed shut without being touched.

Telekenetic. In addition to making pacts with death demons, Wayne Tamarind was a freaking telekinetic. Mother Moon, was I fooling myself to hope that we would make it out of here alive?

"There you are," the voice crooned from a room to the left of the entryway. "We've been waiting for you."

"Well, here I am." Candles flared to life, revealing the dim interior of the room. Wayne sat behind a desk, fingers steepled as though he was about to enter into a business negotiation. Sissy sat bound and gagged on the chaise lounge to his left.

"Let her go." I turned my full attention to the summoner. "You have who you wanted."

"And have her tell the police that I abducted her sister? I think not." His shrewd gaze narrowed, and his voice took on a distinct chill as he snarled, "After what was done to my wife, I don't think I have it in me to do you any favors."

"You were the one who picked up my phone," I said. "You know I had nothing to do with Imogen's death."

"Perhaps," His tone leveled out, gaze narrowing on me. "I've underestimated you before Lily Marie Curtis. I won't do it again."

My name. That had been my name—the bastard had spoken so carelessly. He hadn't dropped it like a bomb, though. That meant I knew something he didn't.

My throat had gone dry, but somehow I kept my voice even as I said, "You're a businessman, aren't you, Wayne? What if I offered you a deal?"

His dark chuckle slithered around me. "And what could you possibly offer me that would be worth risking my reputation?"

"Knowledge," I breathed the word, and my gaze darted to Sissy. Tears tracked down from her blue eyes. Either she was one hell of an actress, or she was in as much danger as I was. My entire escape plan hinged on Azrael showing up for us. "You don't know how I escaped your death demon, do you? What if it happens again? What would that do to your precious reputation?"

I could tell by how his shoulders stiffened that I'd voiced his thoughts.

"You must know I can't let you go," he murmured.

Perhaps there was a way to take Sissy and Draven out of the mix. "I'm not asking you to. I'm asking you to let her go." I jerked my chin toward my sister. "You do and as soon as she's gone, I'll tell you exactly how I am still alive."

Her eyes went wide. She struggled in her chair, almost causing it to tip over as she made sounds of protest that were muffled by her gag. My heart seized up. Yes, I'd been lied to and betrayed, but my instincts were telling me that she was the real deal.

Wayne rose and paced to the fireplace and stared

into the crackling flames. My heart thudded. So many things could go wrong with my plan. He could kill us both outright at any moment. The fact that he hadn't planted a seed of hope in my heart.

Please, please go for it.

Finally, he straightened and then pivoted to face me. When he nodded once, it took all my willpower not to sag in relief.

I sidestepped over to where Sissy sat, tied and protesting. The rope was coarse and had rubbed the thin skin of her wrists raw. My fingers shook as I worked the knot.

The snick of a blade made me freeze. But when I turned it was just Wayne offering me his pocketknife. I could tell by the gleam in his eyes that he didn't think I'd take it. Was it bewitched somehow?

Cautiously, I reached for the handle. Nothing happened when my skin made contact. The fact that he gave me a weapon told me he didn't think I was a threat to him. On my own, he was probably right. But he wasn't counting on my friends.

Keeping track of him out of the corner of my eye, I sawed at the ropes until they fell to the floor. Sissy wasted no time reaching for her gag and tearing it free of her mouth. "Emma, no, you can't do this!"

Before I could protest, Wayne gripped her by the arm and propelled her toward the front door, which opened for him.

"Be careful with her!" I shouted.

He did the opposite, shoving her roughly out the

door and then raising a hand to slam it in her face. I could hear her on the other side as she pounded on it with both fists, screaming my name.

I hadn't seen if Draven made it back outside, but I had to trust he could get her to safety in case my plan didn't work.

"Now," Wayne smirked as he stalked toward me, eyes gleaming. "You know, I should thank you. Imogen was getting on in years. I was already thinking of trading her in for a younger model."

My lip curled in revulsion. "You're a pig,"

"Ah, ah, sticks and stones." He waved the insult aside as his voice hardened. "Now tell me how you survived a death demon."

I had to stall for time to ensure Sissy, and hopefully Draven got away. "First, tell me who hired you to kill me?"

He held up one beefy finger and wagged it back and forth, as though chiding me. An enormous ruby glinted as the bloodred stone caught the firelight. "That wasn't part of our bargain."

"What does it matter though, if you're going to kill me anyhow?"

"It's the principle of the thing," the psychopath muttered.

I'd planned other questions to see if I could get him to confess to Jody Haversham's and Tanya Davis's murders, but the one that tore free was entirely different. "What happened to my baby?"

He blinked. Just once and if I hadn't been looking

for it, I would have missed the gesture. But the question had surprised him. "You didn't even know I was pregnant, did you, you fucking bastard?"

"Enough stalling." He lunged forward and gripped me by my shoulders as though he would shake the answer loose. "Tell me how you survived!"

My chin jutted up as I took a deep breath. "No."

He shoved me, hard. I landed flat on my back and cracked my head on the stone floor. He stalked over to me, hands balled into fists. "You bitch. This time, I'm going to make sure the job gets done."

With that, he twisted the ring on his finger once, twice, and a third time. The room spun as he chanted in a guttural language I'd never heard before. The flames in the hearth surged upward and then reached out, as though hell itself was spitting out the being from its shadowed heart.

Azrael emerged from the fire, black wings flared, and light green irises fixed on me. I trembled at the sight of him—not just for the ruse. He looked like death incarnate as he stalked closer to the two of us.

Wayne's lips parted as though he was on the verge of speaking, but that was when my incubus reached forward and gripped the summoner by the neck, holding the man several feet off the ground.

He didn't look away from his prey as he asked, "Are you hurt, petal?"

"I'm fine," I gasped. "Put him in the chair. I can tie him up—" My words cut off when Azrael stalked back toward the fireplace.

"What are you doing?" I scurried after him.

The incubus tore the ring free from Wayne's finger. Furniture lifted into the air and flew at us as though the entire place was trying to protect its owner. The desk pinned me against the wall, stealing the breath from my lungs as my sore ribs screamed in protest. Azrael's wings sliced through the heavy bookcase that launched at him. The thing fell in pieces as if it were made of wet tissue.

When he glanced over at me, there was real sorrow in his light green gaze. "I'm sorry, Emma, but I must. The next in line demanded a death to add to his tally."

The inferno blazed once more and hands reached out, gripping the sorcerer by the legs. He screamed, the sound one of sheer terror. Azrael released his grip, and Wayne Tamarind was pulled down into the abyss.

I sagged over the desk, defeated. "He had all the answers I needed."

Azrael strode over to me. His dark duster flared out behind him as he moved. He gripped the edge of the desk and sent it spinning into the center of the room. I fell into his arms and cried as he petted my hair.

"You're safe, petal." He breathed into my hair. "You're alive. We'll find out what you want to know."

I sniffed and then pulled back, staring at him as though I'd never seen him before. "You just handed him over to be killed. You didn't tell me it would be like that."

"Emma—"

"No," I shoved him away. "No, I never would have asked for your help if I'd known you would do this."

I was no better than Wayne the pig. And I had nothing to give the sheriff, not even a second-hand confession. Defeated, I covered my face and sobbed.

"I'll be near if you need me," Azrael murmured. My hair blew back as he took flight. Then there was a great crash as he flew through the window. Glass exploded as he soared out into the night.

NINETEEN

"You know there's one thing I don't get," Sissy grunted as we carried my bedframe up the stairs to the apartment I was renting from Mrs. Otis. Hatty and Rue had insisted I take the furniture from my room at Glimmer Ridge "just to get you started, dear."

Moving out was the best thing for all of us. Anger burned in my gut when I thought about them keeping Sissy's identity from me. Another secret. It may have been for my own good, but I wasn't a child. I deserved to know the truth. We all needed space and time to process what had happened.

Of course, nothing with the Bramblewicks was ever simple.

"I'm going to turn your room into a sewing room," Hatty had sniffed.

"You don't sew," Rue pointed out.

"I'll learn." Hatty turned away, nose in the air.

Draven had been right. Everyone kept secrets. I was just sick of them keeping them from me. Of course, I had a doozie of my own.

The image of Wayne being dragged to hell popped into my brain at the worst times. Like when I was carrying a heavy piece of furniture with my sister.

Mother Moon, I have a sister.

"Only one thing?" I refocused on Sissy, and she laughed.

Though bruised and jumpy, she appeared to be recovering well from the abduction. Though Draven transforming from a crow to a naked man had given her pause.

"Honestly, there's a monkey-butt ton that I don't get. But most was that if Wayne killed Jody Haversham and his wife, Tanya Davis, who killed Imogen?"

"No clue." I huffed, my wrapped ribs throbbing as we made the landing. Gasping for breath, I set my end down and straightened. "He thought I did. So did the police, at least until Lou worked her magic, and got me sprung from the slammer."

"Magic being the operative word." Sissy swiped some of her blonde hair away from her face. "She's a witch, you know."

"No, I didn't." Though that explained how she'd convinced the judge to drop the charges so fast. "The question is, how did *you* know?"

"That was how I found you. Through a coven of witches up north. Lou's a cousin to one of the ones I hired to scry for you." She shook her head, blonde ponytail swaying. "It still took them months, even with what felt like a pint of my blood. Never mind all the money for each attempt."

"So why the secrecy?" I asked her. "Why not come to me right away?"

Her tongue darted out as she licked her lips. "You don't remember me, do you?"

Slowly, I shook my head.

She let out a shuddering breath and leaned against the railing. "At first, I had a hard time believing it was you. I kept testing you to see if anything sparked recognition. *The Velveteen Rabbit* was your favorite book as a kid. You used to read it to me."

"And the John Cusack movies?"

Her attention shifted toward the pine trees that surrounded the property, though I got the impression that she didn't see them. "He was always your dream guy."

Before an incubus took the starring role in my dreams.

Her eyes slid shut as she murmured, "I can't believe you don't remember."

"I'm sorry." It hit me again, the weight of it. *I have a sister.* "If it makes you feel any better, I don't remember anyone else from before I came to Mist Glen, either."

She snorted, and when she looked back at me, it was the same lightness of spirit I associated with her. "It really doesn't. We've got a lot of catching up to do. You promised me a pizza in return for manual labor and I fully intend to collect with meatball and onion."

We had already lugged the mattress and box spring up the stairs and all that was left was to figure out how to put the frame together, so it didn't dump me on the floor in the middle of the night.

We traded places, and I stepped over the threshold, walking backward into the studio. The bed would function as my couch. I was used to not having much space and since I'd be spending my days working at *Pages & Potions*, I didn't plan to be at the apartment for more than sleeping.

"Seriously though, who killed Imogen?" Sissy mused as the two of us sat on the floor surrounded by Allen wrenches we didn't have the first clue how to use.

I looked up and saw her worrying her lower lip. "Honestly? Wayne was a contractor for demons. It could have been anyone striking back at him. Hell, for all I know, he lied to me and offed her himself."

That theory, like so many others, didn't sit well. Damn Azrael, I'd needed to interrogate Wayne and get him to confess, so we had something to go on other than endless speculation.

Someone knocked on the door to the apartment. Couldn't be Mrs. Otis. My landlady had made it clear that she never attempted the outdoor steps to the apartment in the winter.

"You invite someone else over?" I asked Sissy.

She shook her head, her blue eyes huge with

worry. I picked up the biggest wrench, ready to clobber anyone who might threaten us even as I hoped my surprise visitor was Azrael.

My heart pounded as I crept closer to the door. I hadn't seen him since that awful day at Wayne's place. Though I'd wanted to apologize for venting all my frustration on him, I hadn't located him on the astral plane. He said he'd be nearby, but I didn't have any way of contacting him. An hour didn't pass without me wondering how he was doing. Where he was living. If he was hungry. Had he found someone else to feed on?

What would it be like to have him in my new apartment instead of in my dreams?

So I hoped, but I wasn't an idiot. After all that had happened, a little extra caution wouldn't hurt.

Wrench held high over my head, I flung the door wide. The man on the other side raised both his dark eyebrows.

Feeling foolish, I lowered my makeshift weapon. "Oh, hey Draven."

"Now is that any way to greet the man who brought you dinner, *cher*?" Draven held a pizza box, his birdlike eyes taking in my new surroundings.

Sissy came up behind me and draped an arm over my shoulder. "You want a warm welcome handsome, you bring a girl chocolates and flowers, not the pie she ordered." Apparently, she had gotten over her apprehension regarding the bird shifter.

He shrugged. "Hey, at least I paid for it. And I

expect a token slice, for true."

Laughing, I stepped back and held the door wide. "Come on in. Maybe you can figure out how to assemble this bedframe."

"Beds are my specialty, you." After landing the pizza box on the counter, he doffed his suede coat and draped it over a barstool. Then he proceeded to sit cross-legged on the ground. Nimble fingers lined up the pieces and tightened the screws until the bed frame stood ready for the box spring and mattress.

"Hot damn." Sissy paused in stuffing pizza into her face to admire his work. "You're a handy guy to have around. That would have taken us all night."

Draven winked and then moved over to the sink to wash his hands. "Don't go spread that around, you. I've worked really hard to make my grandfather believe I'm lazy, for true."

"Your secret is safe with me." Draven's shifting and Azrael's existence weren't my secrets to tell.

Mist Glen would always be a haven for mysteries.

After the pizza was gone, Draven picked up his jacket and caught my eye. "Walk me out, *cher*?"

Behind his back, Sissy made a stupid fanning motion with her hand. I rolled my eyes at her and then snagged my coat off the peg by the door before heading down the stairs.

We didn't speak until we stood by his military-grade vehicle. He didn't seem ready to blurt out whatever was on his mind, so I decided to fill in the empty space.

"Did you get a chance to read the book I gave you?"

He snorted. "I didn't know you were into pedaling smut, you."

In my haughtiest tone, I announced, "I prefer the term cliterature."

That got a laugh out of him. "*Oui*, I read it. And you're right, it was good, though not what I usually read."

"And if you tell me you didn't order the rest of the series, I'll call you a liar."

He held both hands up. "Wouldn't want that." Slowly, his hands fell to his sides. "I was wondering if you would want to go out with me some time, you."

My lips parted, and I blinked at him in stupefaction.

He winced. "The silence says it all, for true." He turned and reached for the car door handle.

Reaching out, I put my hand on his sleeve before he could open it. "You caught me off guard. My life is complicated. And that's not an excuse. Truthfully, it's always complicated."

"She says to the man who turns into a bird." His luscious lips curved up in a wicked smile and those dark eyes drank in my face. "I can handle complicated, you."

Good point. The man changed into a crow so complicated was his comfort zone. He deserved the whole truth. "There's also someone else that I'm kind of involved with. It wouldn't be fair to any of us for me to say yes to you until I make a clean break with him."

"I'm not going nowhere, Emma. You take care of your baggage, and then you call me, for true."

I couldn't help but grin at his confidence. "So sure of yourself?"

"I have a mirror. How could you pass on all this?" He gestured down his body, and I bit my lip to keep from grinning.

When he opened the car door again, I stepped back.

His taillights rounded the bend, heading out to the highway. I didn't know what to think about his offer. He was younger than me, and he turned into a freaking bird. But Draven hadn't lied to me, whereas Azrael...

Turning my thoughts away from men, I headed back upstairs to see if my sister wanted dessert.

"So I disappeared twenty-five years ago?"

Sissy and I lay sprawled across my bare mattress, each of us with a pint of ice cream, talking about a life I couldn't remember.

"Your Sophomore year in college." She rolled to her side and propped her hand under her head. "Honestly, I felt like it was my fault."

"Why?"

She picked at a loose string on the mattress. "We

fought. Mom and Dad were in the middle of breaking up. I was so angry at Dad for stepping out on Mom. It felt like he cheated on the whole family. And when I told you that, you said I needed to get over it. After that, my anger transferred on to you. I called you a narcissist and told you that if that's how you felt about it, you should just stay away from us."

A tear slipped down her cheek. "And then mom got sick. Cancer. It took her fast. By the time you graduated, I didn't have a number for you, had no way of contacting you."

My hand snaked out, and my fingers threaded through hers. "I'm so sorry you went through that all alone, Sissy. If it makes you feel any better, I sound like a real jackass."

Her snort was watery. "Nah. I think you were just as messed up about the whole thing as I was. You handled it differently. I forgave you for that a long time ago."

I squeezed her hand. It was so weird hearing stories about myself. It sounded as if she were talking about a stranger. "And then you went to a coven and had them scry for me?"

"Not right away. I went to college, got married, got divorced. I tried a couple of PIs, but they came up with nothing. A friend finally suggested the coven." She nodded. "It was expensive as hell. Do you know how little money I make as a kindergarten teacher? Took me years to save up." Her gaze met mine, and she whispered, "It was worth it, though."

I had to agree.

"I should get going. Next time you can tell me what you do know." She drew me into an impromptu hug. "I promise, Emma, that no matter what I will help you find out what happened to your baby."

"Thank you," I breathed, holding her tight.

After she was gone, I stripped out of my dirty overalls and stepped into the shower. The water pressure was amazing and thankfully, the water came out hot — no magic required. I took time to blow my hair dry and donned a set of pajamas before unboxing my bed linens and making the bed. I stepped back to enjoy my handiwork when my foot snagged on the barstool. I pitched forward into the wall.

It swung inward.

"Mother Moon." My hands landed on a padded wall. I glanced around the space, stunned. Someone had walled off part of the apartment to make a separate room.

"You found my hidey-hole." The ghost of Jody Haversham appeared behind me. He ran a ghostly hand over the shelf behind me. "I can't believe I forgot about this."

I glared at him over my shoulder. "Your memory lapses are going to be the death of me, Jody."

His smile was weak as tea brewed with a tea bag that had already been dunked twice.

Straightening, I glanced around the space. "What the hell is all this?" The walls and ceiling had been carpeted. A microphone hung from the ceiling and a silver laptop peeked out of a backpack. "It looks like a sound booth."

"It's where I recorded my podcast." He floated over to the bag. "This was my research for upcoming podcasts."

Setting the laptop to the side, I extracted paperback books on witchcraft and Appalachia's history. A massive hardcover that was labeled *Encyclopedia of Demons* was too good to resist, and I pulled it onto my lap.

"Why did you tuck it away like this, though?" I asked as I flipped through the book.

He made a face. "After the business with Wayne, the last thing I wanted was to expose Mrs. Otis to that world. It was easier to pretend to be some sad sack drifter guy in Mist Glen."

I glanced through the pages. "There's a lot here. Maybe something in this mess will help me understand why you haven't crossed over yet."

"Maybe," Jody sighed.

A yawn made my jaw creek. "I'll start looking through it all tomorrow." I rose and reached out toward the door and then froze.

"Emma?"

Pushing the padded door to the hidden room shut, I took in the poster of *The Witching Hour Podcast*. Behind the title, the designer had lavished swirling patterns and symbols that spiraled into infinity. "What is this, Jody?"

"What?" The ghost floated over to my side.

"The pattern in the background. Who thought that up?"

"That? My wife used to doodle those circles on everything. It became a running joke that she could summon me with them. She even had underwear made for me."

All the hair was standing up along the back of my neck. "And who else knew about it?"

His transparent brows drew together. "Well, it was on all the posters for the show, at least after Wayne left. We had T-shirts, buttons, bumper stickers. Stuff like that. I passed them out at conferences and live events. There was a ton of swag in the apartment before I died."

The apartment that had been cleaned out when he'd been missing. My stomach rolled as though it were on a ship at sea.

"Wait, Emma! Where are you going?"

I ripped the poster down, my mind chugging along at a million miles an hour. The show. It all came back to *The Witching Hour*. I needed to get the poster to the sheriff right away—

A big, meaty hand clamped over my mouth and nose. My fingernails reached up, trying to pry it loose. It wasn't until I inhaled that the sharp smell of the chemicals registered. The room spun. I fought, but my limbs wouldn't obey.

Blackness consumed me.

TWENTY

"Wake up, my love." Someone crooned as they stroked my cheek.

My eyelids felt like they'd been glued shut. I lay on a hard surface. The floor? Had I fallen? No, what was beneath my face was colder and rougher than the floorboards in the apartment.

The logy feeling was displaced by the surge of panic-fueled adrenaline that got dumped into my system. The Lair. I was in the Lair. But how?

Though it was a struggle, I forced my eyelids open a crack and looked into the face of Deputy Art Harding.

"You?" I slurred the word.

"That's right, baby," he kneeled back, gifting me the creepiest fucking smile I'd ever seen. "I'm so proud of you, Emma. I've been fighting to free you from their influence for as long as I can remember. They bewitched you. I know they did."

"Who?" I rasped. And then I saw them. Hatty and

Rue were slumped over on the far side of the pentagram. "No!"

Art shushed me. "I know it's hard because they're your cousins. Don't you see? They're evil. They've been trying to turn you against me. But it's finally time for you to be free."

"You're crazy," I breathed. And he laughed. It was a high-pitched, unhinged sound that skittered like bugs over dried bones.

"Crazy for you, baby. You don't have any idea what lengths I've gone to for you, do you?" He reached out to touch my cheek. I jerked away so violently that I cracked the back of my head against the concrete. Stars blurred my vision for a moment.

"Careful. Don't go cracking your skull open. That's not pretty, not at all. That's why I strangled Haversham. It would have been easier to bash his brains in than do all that detail work. But I had to make it look like they did it. That they benefited from carving up a dead man."

I was blowing like a prized Thoroughbred that just won the Kentucky Derby. "And Tanya Davis?"

"Well, the sheriff didn't believe me that the Bramblewicks killed Jody. So I needed another body. Besides, she put you in danger. It was a mercy to put her out of her misery."

"Imogen too?" I croaked.

His countenance darkened. "They dragged you to one of their damn meetings. And that woman attacked you. I thought that would be the one that finally convinced the sheriff to lock them up and throw away the key. But he thought it was you. As if you could hurt a fly, my sweet girl."

"I'm not your sweet anything," I barked.

He just laughed. "Such a lady, always playing hard to get."

"As if." My lizard brain was shrieking at me to shut the hell up. Deputy Art Harding had just confessed to three murders. And he was planning to kill the Bramblewicks, too. If he hadn't already. Damn it, I never should have moved out, shouldn't have left them unguarded. He must have followed them down here.

I could see Rue's chest rising and falling. But Hatty was far too still. "What did you do to them?"

"Added a special ingredient to their tea. It didn't kick in right away. Imagine my surprise when they scurried down here to hunt for an antidote."

A flicker caught my attention. Jody Haversham's ghost wavered beside the Bramblewicks. His transparent gaze took in the situation, met mine for a moment before he vanished.

Much like with the car accident, I was the only one who could see him.

The car accident... "Did you cut the brake line on Hatty's truck?"

He held up both hands. "I never meant for you to get mixed up with that, Emma. I swear to you."

My lips parted. Not the sorcerer. It had been Deputy Crazy Pants all along.

Art was still talking. "Oh Emma, I know this has

been rough on you. I thought you'd be safe in the jail, and I could take care of these two, but that foul-mouth bitch of a lawyer got your case dismissed. If you had just stayed safely in jail, you wouldn't need to see this. Then again, it's better to start with no lies between us. Once you are my wife, they can't compel you to testify against me. We're going to be so happy. You just need to trust me to do the right thing."

Fear made me seize as he extracted a hunting knife from his coat pocket. "What are you going to do to them?"

"Don't worry, baby. No carving. It needs to look like a murder-suicide. This one is dying anyway." He gestured at Hatty's still form.

"What?"

"Didn't she tell you?" Art chuckled. "Heart failure. Doc Trammel gave her six months at most."

I shook my head, refuting the claim even as I recalled her sickly yellow aura, the wheezing breaths, and how tired she seemed lately.

I needed to do something. *Anything*. As he approached my beloved Bramblewicks, I knew time was running out. I was trussed up and couldn't wriggle free. My body hurt all over and the sharp pain every time I drew a breath told me my ribs were a real problem. But he had put me in my coat. The one that still held Wayne Tamarind's pocketknife.

I just needed to get my hands free for a moment...

My head sagged and a moment later I was standing over myself, looking down at my inert form. I stared down at my hands. Like in the astral plane, I appeared solid. Reaching down, I fished in the coat pocket and pulled the knife free. A split second to decide. Free myself or try to stop him in this form? I'd never been astral in the human realm before and didn't know how long I could hold on.

Art crouched over the sisters, muttering to himself. Even if I cut the bonds on my body, there was no guarantee I could get up. Fuck it, I'd take him out as an astral projection.

Or die trying.

My feet made no noise on the concrete floor as I ran for Art Harding. I slammed into him with my considerable weight, leading with the opened blade of the pocketknife. Art stumbled back, hands clutching his throat where the end of the knife protruded.

"Emma!" A rushing sound like a thousand wings barreled down the mushroom stairs. Inky smoke spilled over the floor and then Azrael stood there, wings spread, green eyes blazing.

I felt the pull of my body and let my physical self draw my psychic essence backward.

On my next breath, I lay on my side, hands bound behind me. Art Harding's eyes were sightless as he stared out into the room. Azrael was stumbling to me, his eyes red-rimmed. Sharp talons on the end of one wing sliced my bonds free.

I tried to stand, but my legs had turned to jelly, and my left side was on fire. Crawling on hands and knees,

I made my way over to the Bramblewicks. Their auras flickered with an ominous gray shroud.

"He must have given them something," Azrael breathed.

"Help them." I rasped. "You've got to help them."

He stared at me, his gaze somber. "There's nothing I can do, petal."

"No." I shook my head, unable to believe I could lose both Hatty and Rue in a matter of moments. "No, there must be something."

"Emma," It was Hatty, but when I glanced down at her still body, her eyes remained closed, her chest too still. "Emma, It's okay."

Glancing up, I cried out. Hatty's ghost was the one who spoke to me. My face crumpled.

"Shh, sweetness. It's okay. It's better this way. I was on my way out. You can still save Rue. It's not her time yet. Emma, do you hear me? You can save her."

"How?" I gasped.

"Your sigil. Use your sigil, Emma. Draw it in our circle. Infuse her with your light."

My gaze hunted the archives and fell on chalk. I picked it up and within the pentagram, I drew my symbol. Infinity Ouroboros. Three, four, five times. My hands were steady as I made the seventh and final mark. "Bring her here," I said to Azrael. Gently, the incubus picked up Rue and carried her over to the symbol.

"Now what?" I looked up at Hatty's ghost.

"Blood offering," Hatty breathed. "Use the Athame on the table."

I found the black-handled knife. It bit into my flesh as I drew it across my palm. A line of blood welled. Out of instinct, I knew to press my hand to the outer circle, the one covered with brick dust. Blood dripped. Light flared across the circle, then into the pentacle before finally enveloping my symbol.

Rue arched.

"It's not enough," Azrael breathed.

"It has to be." I didn't know what else I could do.

He turned to face me, his eyes sad. He reached out and caressed my cheek. "Be happy, Emma."

Without warning, he picked up the athame and stabbed it into his chest. His body dissolved and gold glitter mist rained down on top of me, the pentagram, and Rue.

"No!" Too late. He was gone.

"Emma?" Rue sounded groggy. I ran to her and wrapped my hands around her, holding her tightly and sobbing. She was all right. Azrael had made sure that she lived by sacrificing himself.

"It's all right, Emma." Hatty stood over us in her ghostly form. "I promise you that everything will be all right."

And that was when Rue started screaming. She'd spotted her sister's body.

CONTROL FREAK THAT SHE WAS, Hatty had made her funeral arrangements. Her body was to be cremated, and her ashes scattered from the highest peak surrounding Mist Glen.

"So I can keep an eye on everybody." Her ghost, which no longer needed to sniff, did it out of habit.

I shook my head. Rue, her cheeks bright pink from the breeze squeezed my hand and whispered, "Is she here?"

"Tagging along," I muttered. She would know what that meant.

Apart from the two of us, Hatty had only wanted the Dravens, Doc Trammel, Sissy and Mage at her service. The cat was in his carrier, yowling like mad. He'd cheer up later when he realized he wasn't being brought to the vet.

Draven, the elder, held the urn. A stiff breeze blew out of the north. "Rue, you want to do the honors?"

"What, no speeches?" Hatty grumbled.

I snorted, and the younger Draven put a hand on my shoulder and squeezed lightly.

Rue turned to face me, her face tear-stained. "Emma, would you?"

I let out a sigh which hurt my cracked ribs and

then reached out and took Hatty's earthly remains. I turned to face the small, shivering gathering.

"Hatty Eloise Bramblewick was a force of nature. She loved deeply, fought fiercely, and always tried to do what was right."

The ghost nodded her approval, and I smiled a little before continuing. "Everything always had to be her way, but that was because she wanted the very best for everyone around her. She took me in when I had nowhere else to go. I will miss her hugs and even her sharp tongue. Farewell, Hatty. Wherever you are, know that your legacy lives on in the hearts of those who loved you."

"Very nice," Hatty's ghost mumbled and put her transparent hand on Rue's shoulder. Rue shivered and drew her peacoat tighter.

I turned away and lifted the lid to the urn. As though that was the cue it had been waiting for, another gust blew over our heads. I tossed the ashes up into the sky and they soared along the air current, dispersing over the town Hatty loved with all her heart.

The gathering began to head back to their warm cars.

"I never should have left them unguarded," Draven mumbled.

I turned to face him. "Please, don't blame yourself. You had no way of knowing they were still in danger."

"I'm glad you killed the bastard." His dark eyes flashed.

"Me too." Maybe I ought to feel bad about Art Harding's death. Mostly, I was relieved he hadn't become a ghost and hung around to haunt me.

"You okay?" Draven's dark eyes filled with concern.

"I will be."

He drew me into a hug. I almost crumbled. I wasn't thinking of Hatty, who was still with us. But Azrael. Mother Moon, how could he have sacrificed himself that way?

No one else would mourn him. Only I'd known he'd existed.

On the verge of breaking down, I pulled back from Draven's warm embrace. "I think I'll walk back."

He nodded. "If you're sure."

I waited until he was gone before addressing the two apparitions on the hilltop. Jody Haversham and Hatty Bramblewick. "You know I'm the boss of you now," I told Hatty.

Her ghostly gaze narrowed. "You wouldn't dare."

I snorted. "Probably not. Can you see Jody?"

Transparent arms folded over her chest. "Of course I can. I'm dead, not blind."

"The more things change." Shaking my head, I moved stiffly toward the trail that led its way down the mountainside. We'd been walking in silence for several minutes when an odd sort of warmth caught my attention. I turned and then stopped short. Before me, a door appeared but a door unlike any I'd ever beheld. It appeared out of nowhere and light spilled through the widening crack.

"I think this one's for you," I gestured Jody Haversham forward.

The door opened wider, and a woman emerged. She looked so much better than she had in life. No skin sallow from too much booze, no bags beneath her warm brown eyes.

"It's my wife," he breathed. "Tanya."

"Go on," I urged him. "Don't keep her waiting."

That was all it took. Jody dropped his cane and ran for the door. I watched the two of them embrace with a smile. The door eased shut, and the warmth evaporated, leaving only the chill winter wind.

"You weren't tempted to make a break for it?" I asked Hatty.

She snorted. "Someone has to keep you out of trouble."

Petal.

I blinked and realized I'd fallen asleep curled up on the loveseat in Rue's bedroom. My former room lacked a bed. I hadn't wanted to leave the lone Bramblewick sister alone with her grief.

Careful of my ribs, I sat up and tried to work the kinks out of my stiff neck. It was weird, but for a minute there I could have sworn I'd heard Glimmer Ridge, the way I had used to. With a sigh, I trailed my hand across the scuffed wood boards.

Come to me, Emma.

I snatched my hand back. Glanced around. It couldn't be. He'd dispersed. Without making a conscious decision, I pressed my hand to the floor and whispered, "Azrael?"

"I'm here."

My lids slid shut in relief. He was all right. Or at least he hadn't been destroyed. The fog of grief rolled back, and I felt a determination for the first time since we'd left the Lair. I rose and padded barefoot across the chilly boards, careful not to wake Rue. After shutting her bedroom door, I darted into my room and then pressed my back against the door.

The sensation of leaving my body was less jarring than it had been when I'd astrally projected to stop Art Harding. It was a relief to leave my bruised and heartbroken body. My happy cry drowned out the roar of the ocean as I spied Azrael walking toward me down the beach. He was naked once more and his wings were gone. He appeared pale, but those light green irises lit me up from the inside.

I sprinted across the sand and flung my arms around his neck. "How?"

His big palm cupped the back of my head. "It was you, petal. Your rune. Infinity Ouroboros. It returned me to this place."

Sniffling, I pulled away. "Does that mean you're trapped here again?"

The corner of his mouth kicked up. "It appears that way."

I reached for the buttons on my pajama top. "So we'll free you again. Like before."

His hands caught mine before I could disrobe. "No."

"No?" My brows drew together. "Why not?"

He raised our joined hands to his lips and brushed a soft kiss over my skin. "Emma, I want you."

"Still not seeing the problem," I grated.

"I mean in all ways. I want you for my own. To be with you in your world. And you fear me. What I am, what I can do, what I have done. I sense it."

My lips parted to refute his claim. And I couldn't. "You can't stay here, though. You'll starve again."

"Better than to live out there with the pain of not having you." His jaw clenched. "You don't know how hard it was for me to stay away. To abide by your wishes. I deserved to be imprisoned, just for that."

"Azrael, that's crazy." I protested.

"I'm not in pain. It took five years for my energy to deplete to the point of starvation. You don't need to decide right away."

"What are you saying?" I whispered.

He tucked a strand of hair behind my ear. "I want you to go out into the world and live your life. Forget about me."

"Like I could ever," I breathed.

His expression was sad. "I've lived centuries on my

own. I know what the world has to offer. But you, petal, you're just getting started."

"I'm forty-five years old."

"With half a decade of lived experience," he said. "Live your life. If you wish me to be part of it, you know where to find me." He dragged me over to where the hammock swayed in the breeze. He sat and then pulled me down beside him, so our legs dangled over the edge. He pushed the hammock into a rocking motion. "Now, tell me everything that has happened."

He wanted to...talk? Oddly, that felt right, to catch him up on what he missed.

"We called the sheriff and told him the whole story. And Doc Trammel came to patch us up. And to see to Hatty's body," I sniffled, and Azrael squeezed me a little tighter.

"Is her ghost still hanging around?"

A smile stole over my face. "She refuses to leave without her sister, so I don't expect her to go anywhere, anytime soon."

He nodded. "And your apartment? Do you like living elsewhere?"

"I really do. It feels good to stand on my own two feet." I hesitated. "But now that you're back—"

A finger pressed over my lips. "Live your life, petal. I'll always be here when you need me."

"But Rue—"

"Wants what's best for you. I'm sure she's said as much."

He was right—she had.

I laid my hand over his heart. "Thank you for helping me save her."

Those green eyes glowed as he stared down at me. "All I've ever wanted was to see you safe and happy, Emma. That's worth the sacrifice to me."

We were silent then, staring out at the churning waves.

"I can't believe it's over," I sighed and leaned into him.

He kissed the top of my head. "Every ending is also a beginning, petal. Infinity Ouroboros means forever and always."

How right he was.

EPILOGUE

He woke to a soft chime, and the screen of his phone lit the darkened room. He sat up, then reached for the device and read the alert.

Incoming message, code red.

Naked, he strode from his bed and into the bathroom, where he donned a robe. After seeing to his needs, he stalked down the hall to his computer setup. A quick jiggle of the mouse brought the screens surging back to life.

Not bothering to sit, he typed in his code and checked for the nature of the alert. AFIS had flagged something that his web crawlers had detected and signaled as a top-secret file. His fingers flew nimbly over the keyboard as he bypassed firewalls and finally let himself in to see what had triggered his system.

His lips parted at the mugshot that appeared on the screen. It wasn't possible.

And yet it was her. The wide blue eyes, the dark hair that wasn't really curly but not really straight. It was longer than it had been, almost down to her shoulders. He drank in every detail of the unflattering black-and-white image.

"Daddy?" A voice from the hallway drew his attention.

He rounded and then moved out to where his five-year-old son stood. "What's up, Champ?"

"I had a bad dream." The boy swiped the sleeve of his pajamas across his nose.

"Uh oh." Picking the boy up, he headed down the hall to the child's bedroom. After depositing him in the red racecar bed, he drew the blankets up to the child's neck. "Want to tell me about it?"

An abrupt shake of the head.

"Okay then. How about a story?"

"*Peter Pan*," the boy begged.

He reached for the book that sat on the nightstand and started to read. Before Peter got his shadow back, his son had drifted off to sleep.

Setting the book aside, he rose and then returned to his study.

The pixels seemed to waver as she gazed out at him. Though it was a challenge, he read the pertinent details.

"Emma Bishop." His lips twisted in a wry smile. "We'll see each other soon."

To be continued...

*** Note from the author****

THANK you so much for reading. It's my honor to write about midlife heroines, especially with the blend of supernatural adventures and real-world struggles in paranormal women's fiction. And I couldn't do it without you.

Craving more midlife magic? I have some terrific ebook deals for you! Save 15% off the Legacy Witches of Shadow Cove series when you shop at my online store!

AND ...

Save 15% when you buy the full Cougars & Cauldrons series on ebook from my online store.

AND...

Save 15% when you buy the full Silver Sisters series on ebook from my online store.

AND...

Preorder Book 2 My Midlife Magic Knight NOW!

Printed in Dunstable, United Kingdom